Nantucket Heart

A Nantucket Sunset Series

Katie Winters

Chapter One

Very little frightened you after getting a double mastectomy. For Catherine Copperfield, this fearlessness was often difficult to explain to her dearest friends and relatives. They had all slipped easily back into their regular lives and routines after Catherine's brief yet all-encompassing breast cancer in the winter and spring of 2023.

But for Catherine, there was no going back to how things had once been. She wasn't frightened of heights or spiders, nor diving headfirst into projects that had previously riddled her with confusion and dismay. *Cancer changes you*, she thought, *as it should*.

Maybe this fearlessness was what led her to start the book. She'd wanted to write it for years and had threatened Quentin and her sister Sally that she would get around to it *one of these days* for the better part of the past twenty. But now, her youngest kid was in his senior year of high school, her middle daughter was at college, and her eldest daughter was living on her own—so Catherine had more time than she knew what to do with. More time to think.

Had she known what would come of writing that book, maybe she would have been frightened.

But there was no one left to warn her.

"It's a deep dive into my family's history," Catherine explained at a party one night. "How we came to be the way we are; how we got to America; what our past was like."

She was at The Copperfield House with Quentin's tremendous family and the current iteration of artists-in-residence. It was early August, not long after Alana and Jeremy's wedding, and everyone was in good spirits. Spread out across the back porch, they drank wine or light beers as the bright orange sun dunked into the Nantucket Sound. A few of the kids splashed in the waves along the shore, erupting with laughter. Soon, they would be called in to eat—but not yet. They would cling to every bit of summer they could.

Catherine's mother-in-law, Greta, leaned back in her chair and swirled her wine in its glass. She seemed to be rolling over what Catherine had just said. At least, that was what Catherine hoped. It was often hard to read Greta's mind. She was a wildly intelligent individual, a few notches ahead of Bernard, and only said what she thought when it suited her. Because Quentin hadn't spoken to any of his family prior to spring 2022, Catherine was still building relationships and getting to know the ins and outs of the family. She was fascinated with them. But she also dreaded the day Greta Copperfield sniffed and said Catherine's idea for a book was a bad one. What would Catherine do, then? Greta was a literary prodigy!

"I've always found nonfiction difficult," Greta said. "But I have to imagine that most nonfiction books require a hint of fiction. You have to fill in the gaps that you just don't know. Do we really know what famous historical figures ate on a given afternoon? Do we really know what they listened to when they got ready for battle? No. But we fill in the gaps based on historical context. We paint a picture of what it might have been like as a way to describe how it really was. As a way to relate to it from where we sit now."

Catherine felt the intellectual slant of Greta's tone and stiffened her shoulders. Although she'd already had half a glass of wine, she wanted to be up for this kind of conversation. She wanted to be ready to show Greta her chops.

"So my question to you is," Greta said, "why not fictionalize the story? Write about you and a version of your family that's 'almost' correct but with flourishes here and there. It's far more sellable that way."

Catherine winced, thinking of her mother and her father and the tremendous stories they'd passed on to her. "I want to get the stories exactly right. I want to honor my family. You know, I'm a journalist by trade. Fiction just isn't in my wheelhouse."

"But the stories themselves are probably not correct," Greta pointed out. "Things get lost along the way. I could tell you a story about Bernard and me in Paris many years ago, and the things I told you wouldn't be one-hundred-percent correct."

Catherine bristled, thinking of her father's massive hands, her mother's kind eyes, and the laughter that echoed in the kitchen of her childhood home. The stories her parents had told her had been true; they couldn't be anything else. They belonged to them. They were their currency.

Catherine resented that Greta said they weren't true, although she understood what Greta meant. Catherine wet her lips. What could she say now?

Suddenly, Scarlet appeared on the porch in a red swimsuit and a pair of cutoffs. Her hair was salty and curly and wild, and she wore a shade of red lipstick that spoke of the carefree nature of her twenty-four years on earth, her startling bravery as she built her career as a documentarian, and the clear fact that she now lived on her own in Nantucket—in an apartment she rented herself. Catherine had never even been inside it before. Scarlet had insisted on doing everything herself.

It was never clear to Catherine how much longer Scarlet would live in Nantucket. She had wonderful connections via her father, of course, and Catherine knew Scarlet adored working alongside her father on his numerous projects. But the problem was clear. If Scarlet remained here, she would forever work and live in her father's shadow. And if she went somewhere else—back to New York City or Los Angeles or Seattle or Atlanta—she could build a career on her own merit. She would stand on her own name.

"There's my darling girl," Greta said, reaching for Scarlet's hand. "Your mother was just telling me about her latest project."

Scarlet's eyes shimmered. She glanced up at her mother with a secretive smile. Catherine had only shared bits and pieces of her family history with Scarlet, as the immensity of the stories often overwhelmed even Catherine. But that was one of the reasons she wanted to write the book. She wanted everything out in the open.

She wanted Scarlet and her other children to know the ins and outs of it. If it were published for a wider audience, that would be great. But Catherine couldn't have cared if the only bookshelf the novel ever saw was her own.

"We're going to Ellis Island soon," Scarlet announced to Greta. "Mom wants to search for her family's signature."

Greta cocked her head. "For the book, I presume?"

"Yes," Catherine said.

"And you know what you're looking for?" Greta asked.

"Yes," Scarlet answered for her mother. "Mom's grandfather came to the States in the early forties. Right, Mom? And he was really important. Back home in Italy, he'd owned swathes of land and a couple of castles."

Greta's eyes sparkled with intrigue. Catherine cursed herself. *I should have started with the castles. I bored her earlier. Scarlet has a better handle on how to entice her audience—just like her father.*

"My goodness! Why haven't you mentioned this?" Greta asked.

"What's going on?" Quentin approached with a negroni and a cube of cheese and looked from his mother to his wife to his eldest daughter. It was clear from his expression that he was pleased they were all together, three of the people he loved most in the world.

"Your wife just shared that she's related to Italian royalty," Greta said. "I can't believe I never knew!"

Quentin bent to plant a kiss on Greta's cheek. "Can't you see it written all over her face?" he asked. "She's my Italian queen." Suddenly, Quentin switched into an Italian-inspired Super Mario accent and said, "That's why she demands nonstop pasta and cheese and focaccia! It's never-ending! I'm constantly cooking, Mama!"

Catherine whacked him on the shoulder. Greta and Scarlet giggled.

"If only you cooked me nonstop Italian food," Catherine said. "I'd love it."

"You know my limitations," Quentin pointed out. "I know my way around the microwave, and that's about it."

Bernard announced it was time for steak: bloody and gorgeous slabs of well-spiced meat, grilled onions and zucchini, potato salad, and fresh bread. Catherine hurried over to grab a plate and joined her three children and Quentin at a picnic table stretched across the sand. From inside, someone turned up the speaker system, and The Doors' Jim Morrison crooned across the beach.

Greta called to everyone with her glass raised, "One more month of summer! Let's make the most of it, Copperfields! We love you!"

Everyone raised their glasses happily. Catherine's heart jumped into her throat. It was times like these—times of joyousness with family, times when she was seated with her three children and her husband, times that felt so normal—that Catherine remembered how close she'd been to death. It had shadowed her for months. Sometimes Catherine had been so frightened to leave her children and husband behind that she'd stayed up late, staring into the darkness over her and Quentin's bed, fearful that if she fell asleep, she wouldn't wake back up.

That had been before her surgery and before they'd come to Nantucket. Something about Manhattan had pressed in on her from all sides. It had suffocated her.

It had been a city she'd adored for decades. It had been home.

Then very suddenly, it was not.

Once, during that very dark time of chemotherapy, trauma, and hair loss, Catherine reached out to a therapist. She didn't want to burden her children or her husband with too many of her horrible emotions; she didn't want to worry them. So she told the therapist everything that was on her mind.

"This is a good start," the therapist had said after an hour. "But we need to do this once a week to make any real progress."

"Once a week?" Catherine hadn't been able to believe it. She'd thought she would die soon. She didn't have time to fix her mind.

Now, a year and a half later, she wasn't frightened of anything. But she wasn't fully mentally healed either.

More than anything, she wanted answers to her family's great questions.

She wanted to live.

And she felt as though this book would cure her far more than any therapist might.

After dinner, they cleared the plates, moved aside the picnic tables, and had an impromptu Copperfield dance party along the beach and the bright green lawn. Catherine laid her head on Quentin's shoulder and swayed in time to "It Had to be You," watching the other couples do the same: Greta and Bernard, Alana and Jeremy, Julia and Charlie, Ella and Will, Aurora and Brooks. Scarlet was off to the side, whispering in Ivy's ear. *What is she talking about?* Catherine wondered. *My children are mysteries to me.*

"How do you think our girl is doing?" Catherine breathed into Quentin's ear.

"Which one?"

"Your protegée," she answered.

Quentin's eyes widened. "She's been brilliant."

"Does she ever talk about getting bored here?"

Quentin sighed. "I know you want our kids to grow up as soon as possible. But I like that she's here. I have plenty of work for her to do, and she comes to all of James's games, and she knows her grandmother, and—"

Catherine cut him off. "I hope she knows she has just this one life to do everything she wants to do."

Quentin arched his eyebrow.

"I just don't want her to be frightened of change," Catherine said, backing down. "I regret every day I was frightened as a young woman."

"You? You were never frightened of anything!" Quentin said. "I still remember how difficult you were in the newsroom. You were so argumentative. If you thought you had a killer story, it didn't matter what the editor said. You were going to write it. And he always, always published it. Even if he'd said no during the pitch round."

Catherine giggled at the memory. It was true that when she'd met Quentin, she'd been incredibly aggressive, bright, and quick on her feet—all elements required for a gig in the field of journalism. When he'd first come along, she'd been in the midst of cracking a case about corporate greed. The case itself had gone national, and the corporation in question had fired their CEO and tripled their efforts for equal pay between the sexes, better treatment of mothers and fathers, and even better pay for entry-level positions. With those frantic few weeks of work, Catherine liked to think that she'd changed the trajectory of hundreds of people's lives.

Ten years after the story broke, the corporation had gone under. Catherine hadn't known what to feel. Had she been instrumental in destroying that corporation and thus many, many jobs? Or was there too much toxicity at the root of the company in the first place? Maybe the new CEO still demanded too much. Perhaps there was no room for generosity in a place built like that.

Still, Catherine ached to think of the workers who'd had to re-enter the endless process of applying and interviewing and hoping.

Would it have been better for them to keep their jobs, even if the workplace wasn't fair?

Catherine was plagued with questions.

More than anything, she was overwhelmed with guilt for their tremendous wealth. She tried to remember to be grateful. Despite her past as an "Italian princess," her family had lost everything upon coming to America, and she'd grown up quite poor. Perhaps that was another reason she wanted to dig into her family's backstory. *So much trauma passed down.*

Because Catherine was Catherine Copperfield—and, therefore, Quentin Copperfield's wife—she hadn't worked straight through her career the way other journalists had had to. She'd dipped in here and there with a freelance assignment; she'd never let her writing chops rust.

But now that she had the time and the fearlessness and the open heart to finally try, she was eager to get to the bottom of her family history and write about what they'd left behind in Italy.

She couldn't wait to get her hands dirty in the mess of her family's life.

And she was so thrilled that Scarlet wanted to help her, too.

Maybe they would bond all over again, the way they had during the chemotherapy.

Maybe Catherine would find a way to impart to Scarlet how essential these years were. *You're descended from Italian royalty. You're not just a Copperfield. You need to meet your destiny.*

Later that night, as Catherine tugged on her cardigan and hugged Greta goodbye, Greta whispered in her ear, "I can't wait to read your book, darling. Good luck at Ellis Island. Not all of us are lucky enough to understand the dramatic stories of our roots. But you're a brilliant researcher. Whatever there is to know, you'll find it."

Catherine's heart felt like a balloon. She'd thought Greta didn't approve of her book. Later, Quentin said, *She just likes to have an opinion. That's my mother for you.*

Catherine tugged Scarlet's hand along with her. She was thrilled that Scarlet had agreed to spend the night at the family home in Siasconset rather than return to her dinky little apartment to eat potato chips and watch YouTube. Catherine liked nothing more than having all her children under one roof.

Safe in the car, Quentin turned the key and drove them back through an impenetrable dark night. The garage door went up, and very soon, they were all nestled on the sofa and chairs, and the blue glow of the television fell over them. James cracked open a soda, Scarlet painted her toenails, and Ivy made popcorn. Quentin drew his arm around Catherine's shoulders and held her close.

Catherine's heart thudded with gratefulness. *I still have my life. I still have my life.*

Chapter Two

The following morning, Scarlet woke up in the bedroom she and Ivy shared when they stayed with their parents. It was painted lilac with soft, fluttery white curtains, which they agreed was far more suitable for ten-year-olds than women their age. Their mother hadn't yet decided what to paint it, not since they'd purchased it last year, and Ivy and Scarlet both understood that their mother wanted to pretend they were little girls just a while longer.

But Scarlet knew it thrilled Ivy to be home for the summer, and Scarlet adored spending so much time with her little sis—someone far different from Scarlet, who was becoming more and more like an adult every day.

Sometimes it scared Scarlet to think that she and Ivy might one day not see eye to eye. That they might spend *twenty-five years apart,* the way their father and aunts had. It sounded ludicrous. How had they allowed that to go on?

Ivy was tan and athletic and sporting a romance with an islander that she was keeping a secret from their parents. Ivy often pestered Scarlet about why she wasn't dating. "That whole Owen thing was years ago," Ivy liked to say.

"But it wasn't," Scarlet insisted. "It was a year and a half ago. I can't just bounce back like that."

Owen was Scarlet's long-term boyfriend who'd not only cheated on her but had also stolen thousands and thousands of dollars in both goods and cash from her. They'd caught him red-handed on the evening news. In one fell swoop, Scarlet's relationship and faith in men had fallen apart.

The breakup had mended Scarlet's relationship with her father—a man she hadn't been able to stand prior to. This had surprised her at the time.

Quentin had been very vocal about his dislike for Owen, but he hadn't rubbed news of how seedy he was into her face. It was part of the reason they'd been able to move on so well as a family.

But Scarlet had been eager to replace her reliance on men with her love of her career. Immediately, she'd launched herself into the sphere of documentarians, helping her father with everything from building stories to interviewing to holding the camera to sending emails. There were also many parties to attend—evenings in which they "hobnobbed." Quentin was incredible at it; people fawned over him because they knew his face so well from the evening news. It was almost as though they felt they had ownership over him. Scarlet sometimes had to bite her tongue to keep from saying, *You don't know him at all.*

But of course, Scarlet's mother was always dancing around the idea of: *Don't you want to make your own documentaries? Don't you want to step outside of your father's shadow?*

The truth was, Scarlet did. But she was too terrified to explain her idea. Her mother was a brilliant researcher and journalist, and her father was Quentin Copperfield, for crying out loud. Scarlet's first attempt was bound to be bad. And she sort of wanted it like that. She wanted to make mistakes. She wanted to see if she was actually worth anything on her own.

Ivy was still asleep, sprawled over the top of her comforter with her mouth flung open. It wasn't a good look. Scarlet tiptoed to the bathroom, then hurried downstairs to pour herself a cup of coffee. She heard her mother and father in the next room, talking about the specifics of Catherine and Scarlet's trip to the city tomorrow. Catherine had already booked a hotel, and Quentin told her she should have booked another one because he knew the owner and could have gotten her a better deal. Scarlet rolled her eyes and retreated upstairs to her notebook.

This was what she liked to do every morning.

She liked sitting in bed with her coffee and researching her documentary on her phone. She made notes to herself, fleshed out more of the concept, and made lists of potential locations to shoot and possible people to interview. The story was barely anything right now, and everything was a crapshoot. But it felt nice to get it out on the page.

She'd learned a great deal over the previous year-plus of working with her father. But she didn't want her documentaries to have the same tone as his. His were featured on The History Channel; they were sure of themselves and formulaic. Scarlet wanted hers to be more fun and stylish, more from the heart and soul of a twenty-four-year-old girl. She didn't think that was too much to ask for.

She'd gotten the idea earlier this summer.

Scarlet had been on the fence at the time. Heavy with indecision, she'd considered moving back to the city, or moving across the country, or continuing her strange and uninspiring life in that very room at her parents' place—helping her mother repaint various rooms and organize the new kitchen.

Scarlet had met her dear friend Alyssa Potter for coffee one morning in June. Scarlet and Alyssa grew up together in the city—both with arguably difficult fathers and too much money and privilege, but now, they lived in Nantucket and Martha's Vineyard, respectively, after heaps of changes in their respective lives. A big difference between them was that Alyssa's father had cheated on her mother and left her for her mother's best friend. Another big difference was that Alyssa's father had died of a heart attack not long after that—and left the entire family reeling. *How do you forgive someone who's already dead?* Scarlet had often wondered.

Alyssa now had a baby and a husband—a funny thing for a young woman who'd been so much of a wild vagabond during her twenties. In her white dress with her baby asleep against her chest, she looked beautiful and innocent. Scarlet struggled to know what to say. She was thrilled for her, of course. But they were also on two very different roads of life. Scarlet wondered if Alyssa thought Scarlet didn't have her life together anymore. She wondered if Alyssa was secretly judgmental.

I'm only twenty-four! Scarlet had wanted to scream.

But that was when three young women entered the

coffee shop. They were a little bit younger than Alyssa and Scarlet, wearing long dresses that hid their feet. They had big sleeves and long hair that went past their waists. The only thing different about them was their facial features and hair color—proof they weren't related, or only very distantly.

They purchased tea and sat directly on the floor in a circle, cross-legged. Scarlet had never seen anything like it. Her heart had thumped. They'd taken each other's hands, closed their eyes, and said a prayer that Scarlet couldn't quite hear.

Scarlet and Alyssa ignored them for a while after that. Scarlet dismissed them as very religious people; maybe they didn't believe in chairs or something. What did she know?

She would have forgotten the entire thing were it not for what happened next.

The girls got up and headed for the door. But one of them caught Scarlet's eye, and she looked harder.

"Melanie?" Scarlet stood with surprise. The girl with the darkest hair was her sister Ivy's friend from high school. Scarlet was one hundred percent sure of it because Ivy had had her over what felt like thousands of times, and they'd always stolen Scarlet's makeup.

Melanie stopped short and gaped at Scarlet. All the color drained from her face. It was like she didn't want to be caught.

Does Melanie's family have a place around here? Didn't she go to university? What is happening? Scarlet thought.

Another girl grabbed Melanie's hand and dragged her out before Melanie had a chance to speak. But Scarlet had had the sense that Melanie didn't want to admit her name.

It was eerie.

Scarlet had asked Ivy about Melanie immediately via text. Ivy had said she hadn't heard from Melanie, and she hadn't updated her social media in a while. When Scarlet had mentioned seeing Melanie in "a super long skirt and no makeup, almost like she was in a cult," Ivy had said, "Melanie went to Princeton. She was a perfectionist. There's just no way it was her."

But Scarlet had been sure.

Now, she was on a quest. Who were those girls? What were they up to? Why were they wearing that?

She'd been hard at work on this research for months, but she still hadn't gotten far. Her only "clues" involved a rumor she'd heard—that another girl around Ivy's age had "left college under mysterious circumstances." That, and she'd seen two other girls in town wearing similar clothing. But she'd gone through endless social media posts. She'd read Reddit till she was blue in the face.

But this morning was different.

Yesterday before the party at The Copperfield House, Scarlet had left a post on a Reddit thread, asking if anyone had any information about the "girls in conservative hippie clothing." She'd expected it to be ignored like everything else.

This morning, there was a comment.

Scarlet's heart stopped beating.

A user named alfieomalie17 had written: I've seen them doing something weird on Miacomet Beach a few nights this summer. It's creepy that the girls dress like that, but the guys dress weird, too.

Scarlet gaped at it. Her thoughts whirred. Before she could stop herself, she responded.

Scarjar12: Is there a pattern for when they're there? Can you describe what the men wear? Do you get the sense they're dangerous?

But a few seconds later, her comment, the user's comment, and the entire thread were deleted. Scarlet got out of bed and stared at her phone. Her notebook sat sadly on her sheets.

Somebody doesn't want me to read that, she thought. *But why?*

Chapter Three

Catherine hadn't returned to New York in six months. Seeing the skyline through the car window sent cold chills down her arms and legs. It was the same skyline that had called to her grandfather over gray and blue waters as the giant vessel made its final lurch to America. She wondered what it was he'd felt. Relief? Gratefulness? Or had he longed for his golden Italian hills, his turquoise Mediterranean waters?

Catherine had been to Italy only a couple of times, and both had been overscheduled and action-packed with all things Quentin's career. He'd had to meet other newscasters; he'd had to conduct interviews with famous movie stars and fashion models and so on. Catherine had been shuffled around with royalty, thinking only of her grandfather, of the man who'd once felt such prominence on the same soil. Once or twice, Catherine had considered staying in Italy to conduct more research about her grandfather's past. But back then, she'd had younger children and hated leaving them in the city with a nanny or a friend.

Scarlet was mysteriously quiet during the ride. A few times, Catherine prodded her with questions, asking her about her ideas for a documentary, asking if she needed anything for her new apartment. Catherine knew she sounded overwhelmingly "mother-like," but she couldn't help it. Scarlet's silence was worrisome.

"Are you going to try to meet up with any old friends while we're here?" Catherine asked as they crossed the bridge into Manhattan.

"I don't know. Alyssa's in Martha's Vineyard, and I haven't kept in touch with many others."

Catherine's heart twinged at the mention of Alyssa Potter. Alyssa had a husband and a child. She owned and operated a bakery slash bookstore in Martha's Vineyard with her sister Maggie. She had a small but beautiful life. Her mother, Janine, was probably so proud.

I need to give Janine a call, Catherine thought for the thousandth time. But lives moved forward so quickly. Before you knew it, you hadn't talked to people you loved in years.

Catherine gave the hotel valet driver her keys and watched as the bellhops gathered their suitcases and wheeled them into the lobby. This was the sort of high-society city life they'd once taken for granted. But Catherine wasn't accustomed to it now. Her fingers itched with the desire to handle her things herself.

The hotel clerk gave them their keys—a room for Scarlet and a room for Catherine with a central room in the middle that they shared. They went upstairs and spent a few minutes in their room to tidy up and take a bit of time for themselves. Catherine closed her door and wondered what Scarlet did in her room. Probably texting? That was what twentysomethings did, right? Thinking of it, Catherine sent a text to Quentin to say they'd arrived safely.

QUENTIN: Good luck! Can't wait to hear all about Ellis Island!

But Catherine and Scarlet weren't due for Ellis Island till tomorrow morning. They'd made an appointment at nine thirty so they could have sufficient time alone with the book he'd signed and, hopefully, the photograph they'd taken of him at the time—a routine procedure during 1942.

Funnily enough, Ellis Island ceased operation in 1943—just one year later. It meant Catherine's grandfather was one of the final people Ellis Island had welcomed.

I wonder what they thought of this high-society man from Italy entering the gates of Ellis Island just like everyone else.

Catherine was to be the first person in her family to go to Ellis Island and see his signature. She was the first to dig into the familial stories that served as the backdrop of future generations.

For that evening, Catherine had made dinner reservations at a beautiful restaurant near Central Park—one where they'd celebrated numerous family birthdays over the years. Even Scarlet's eyes lit up when Catherine shared the plans. A few hours before dinner, mother and daughter stepped out for a stroll in a city they both knew deep in their bones. They strode up toward Central Park, gossiping about the past and the people they'd once known.

"I hope we run into Tess Hedges," Scarlet said under her breath, speaking of an old neighbor of theirs on the

Upper West Side. "She always said the strangest things when we ran into her. Remember that time she told us she was looking for gold beneath her house in the Hamptons?"

Catherine giggled and smacked her hand over her mouth.

"Come on," Scarlet said. "You remember."

"I do."

"Did she ever find it?"

"Well, last I heard, she got a nose job," Catherine said.

"I guess she found the gold, then!"

Catherine's smile was so big it hurt her face. She'd forgotten about poking fun at the vanity of the Upper West Siders.

"Does it look good?" Scarlet asked.

"What?"

"The nose job!"

"Oh. Um. I think she went too small!" Catherine said.

Scarlet giggled and linked her arm through her mother's. Warmth flooded Catherine's arms and legs.

Catherine remembered the first time Scarlet had gossiped with her. Scarlet had been twelve or thirteen, and they'd seen a woman in an elaborate purple fur coat stroll down Park Avenue. "What's that peacock doing over there?" Scarlet had asked. And Catherine had burst into peals of laughter so great that she'd had to hide in a lobby of a community center.

She's not just my daughter, she thought. *She's my friend, too.*

It was a rejuvenating feeling.

It was true you saw all kinds of people in the city. It

was a different cast of characters than Nantucket Island—people from all over the world, dressed in all manner of things, going who-knew-where. It was a Wednesday, but that didn't mean the city was any less alive than it was on the weekend.

"I took you there when you were little," Catherine said as they passed a little place where girls could pick out dolls and choose their outfits and call them by whatever name they wanted. "I still remember the way you looked at the doll you made. You called her 'Rachel,' and you said she was going to change your life."

Scarlet laughed. "It's funny. I don't think I even knew I had a cousin named Rachel back then."

"You didn't," Catherine said.

"Did you think about telling me right then?"

Catherine thought for a moment, remembering the complexity of keeping their children out of the mess of the Copperfield family. "It felt like a different dimension to ours entirely," Catherine said. "Rachel was all the way in Chicago with Julia. We lived here. I never imagined in a million years your father would reunite with his family."

Scarlet's eyes caught the glow of the low-hanging street lamps as they turned on that early evening. "Are you happy we moved to Nantucket?"

"I'm blissfully happy," Catherine admitted, feeling her heart melt. "But when we're in the city, all these memories come flooding back. I can't fight them."

"I feel the same way," Scarlet said.

Before dinner, Scarlet and Catherine went to a swanky cocktail bar on a rooftop in the Upper West Side. It was brand new, something Scarlet had seen on social media, and from the top, they could make out one of the windows of the home where Catherine and Quentin had raised their babies. A shiver ran down her spine. The new owners had closed the drapes, but had they not, she might have been able to peer into the little room she'd once used as her office. How many articles had she written in that room? How many private cries had she had, wondering how she was going to make it as a journalist and as a mother and as the famous Quentin Copperfield's not-so-famous wife?

But she was forty-eight now. She'd beat cancer. Her children were almost all out of the house. Did that mean she'd made it?

Catherine turned to catch a young man approaching Scarlet with a beer in his hand. He smiled at Scarlet, who flinched away from him. Catherine's heart darkened. The young man attemped a conversation, but Scarlet reeled back and gestured toward Catherine. The man left, shoulders dropped, and Scarlet returned to Catherine with a loose smile that Catherine didn't believe for a minute.

"Did you know that young man?" Catherine asked.

"What? No." Scarlet's tone was harsh.

"Did he want to buy you a drink?"

"I guess."

"You could have let him," Catherine said. "It's always fun to meet new people."

Scarlet half rolled her eyes.

"All right. Sorry I said anything." Catherine inhaled.

Scarlet sighed. "Sorry. I just wasn't interested. Is that okay?"

"Of course it is." Catherine pressed her lips together and remembered Owen. Maybe Scarlet couldn't trust men anymore because of him. Catherine certainly couldn't blame her if so.

Scarlet tucked her jet-black hair behind her ear and

glanced at the floor. The DJ switched, and the pleasant electronic beats transitioned to something harder.

"Let's head to the restaurant," Catherine suggested.

"Sounds good."

It was a brilliant night, save for that single hiccup. Over Italian food, Scarlet and Catherine laughed and joked about the past; they talked about how much they were going to miss Ivy when she returned to the city; they talked about James's surprise jock career after his move to Nantucket and the clear truth that he was the most popular kid in school. They talked about Quentin's latest documentary at the Sunrise Cove Inn and how it had assuredly revolutionized how people thought about Martha's Vineyard.

"I can't get over that the Underground Railroad went right through there!" Scarlet whispered, her fork rotating over her pasta.

Eventually, Catherine returned to the topic of her family and her book. "Maybe it's just me getting old, but I want to make sense of myself in the context of my family," she said. "When I got sick, I thought of all these relatives I've heard about. They lived, and they loved, and they had children, and they worked, yet they're all gone now. Someday, I'll be gone, too."

Scarlet gave her a look that meant *don't*.

But Catherine pressed on. "I fought hard for the life I still have. You were there with me every step of the way, and I can't thank you enough." Catherine reached across the table to take Scarlet's hand. "One day, I want your granddaughter to know about us. I want them to understand where we came from and what my grandfather gave up. I want this all to be connected through time and space. And that's why I want to fight so hard to write this book. It's my mark."

Scarlet's eyes glinted with tears. "I get it, Mom," she said softly. "You didn't need to explain."

Catherine laughed at herself and tapped her napkin beneath her eye. "I know," she whispered. "But sometimes I have to explain my obsession to myself, too."

Chapter Four

Catherine woke up at six the following morning and left the hotel to jog around Central Park. It was already a sunny morning, but not even seventy degrees yet, and her muscles felt spry and bouncy as she swept through the trees, taking deep breaths. She passed other joggers and slender women pushing strollers in which sleeping babies lay. The babies had no idea what sort of life they'd been born into: a life of incredible privilege; a life in Manhattan; a life to a mother who cared so much about herself and her children that she woke up at the crack of dawn and put herself through the wringer to pay her bills and meet the right people and get her kids into the perfect daycare and preschool and elementary. It was a rat race. And it didn't end till they went to college.

Catherine's race was mostly over. She inhaled deeper, realizing that back when she'd been in the midst of those early years, she'd hardly managed to breathe at all.

Catherine paused to stretch on a patch of lush grass and extended her neck to look at the wide blue sky overhead. The city was coming to life, its horns blazing, its subways chugging along under her feet. She felt a deep and unending gratitude.

This is what you came here for, she said to her grandfather up there in the sky. *I hope I carry your legacy well.*

Catherine returned to the hotel by seven to find Scarlet still in bed with a notebook propped across her thigh and her phone out. She made notes frantically with a black pen.

"What's up?" Catherine asked from the crack in the doorway. She glistened with sweat.

Scarlet nearly jumped out of bed with surprise. "I didn't hear you come in."

Catherine laughed and pulled her hair from its ponytail. Scarlet closed her notebook and fixed her face. It was clear whatever she wrote was nothing she wanted to share.

Maybe she's working on a secret project, Catherine thought hopefully. *Perhaps she'll clue me in when the time is right.*

"How was your run?" Scarlet asked.

"It was gorgeous. I fantasized about moving back."

Scarlet wagged her eyebrows. "You're a city girl!"

"Not anymore," Catherine said with a sigh.

Catherine showered and came out to find a big pot of black coffee in the room between their bedrooms. Scarlet was showered and dressed in a trendy suit jacket with a pair of black shorts. She looked both professional and beautiful. Where had she learned to do that?

Catherine assembled everything required for the day ahead—a professional Canon camera, her phone, her laptop, and her notebook—and put them in her leather backpack. Scarlet packed a smaller backpack with her personal items and filled a water bottle. By eight, they were out the door to grab another cup of coffee from a local joint on the corner. In line, they watched a woman in her thirties lose her mind at the cashier because he'd put regular milk in her latte when she'd specifically asked for oat.

Scarlet and Catherine winced and made faces at each other.

"Okay," Catherine breathed, "maybe I'm not fantasizing about moving back anymore."

It was rare to see that behavior in Nantucket, at least among locals. An occasional city person lost their head with the waitstaff, but often, they were able to cool off and have an okay time a few minutes later. They were on vacation, after all.

Catherine and Scarlet took a cab to Battery Park. There, they lined up for the ferry and took plastic seats up on top. Catherine wanted to take photos as the island got closer and closer. She wanted to feel as close to her grandfather as she could.

Catherine and Scarlet reached Ellis Island fifteen minutes later. The second Catherine's feet found the concrete on the island, a shiver went through her entire body. *This is hallowed ground,* she thought. *This is where everything changed.*

But where did his money go?

How did he lose it?

Catherine's search was ripe with questions. Surely, there would be a clue here in Ellis Island. Indeed, this was an essential step.

Because Catherine and Scarlet had made an appointment, they could enter the records building before the other tourists. A curator named Deb met them and shook their hands. She had a sharp blond bob and very white teeth and spoke eloquently about Ellis Island in the manner of someone who gave the same speech every day but never really tired of it.

"How long have you been working here?" Catherine asked as they followed Deb deeper into the records area.

"Twenty years," Deb answered. "It was my dream to work in museums, but Ellis Island is next-level. It's more interactive. People like you come with questions about their family and their past. It's remarkable what we learn together. We fill in gaps. We rewrite history together."

Catherine hurriedly scribbled what Deb had just said on her notepad. Deb needed to be in her book somewhere. Maybe she could interview her at a later date; perhaps she could ask questions about Deb's journey to curatorial work or her opinion about immigration or hear about the worst and best stories here on Ellis Island.

But this morning was all about Catherine's relative: Gionnocaro Fellini.

"It was 1942, correct?" Deb asked.

"Yes. September 1942. One year before you closed down," Catherine confirmed.

They'd paused in front of the mighty collection of books. They were as thick as tomes, with hundreds of brown and yellow pages upon which immigrants from mostly Europe had arrived and filled in their names and occupations. Because Catherine's grandfather had come so much later than the initial gush of immigrants, his section included photographs. Catherine couldn't wait to see his innocent and big-eyed face, assuredly so fearful about the coming months of hardship.

"Here we go," Deb said as she put on a pair of gloves and proceeded to carefully go through the pages from September 1942. Catherine couldn't breathe. She took numerous photos of the photos of immigrants and their occupations: baker or steelworker or dressmaker or architect. Her heart felt bruised at the expression on their faces. Fear. Turmoil. Because it was 1942, many of them had escaped the war in Europe. Maybe some of them were Jewish; perhaps they were running away from certain death.

Deb searched and searched and searched. However, after going through the entirety of September 1942, they found no sign of Gionnocaro Fellini.

Catherine's thoughts spun.

"You're sure it was September?" Deb asked.

Catherine nodded. It was family lore: September 1942. No question.

Deb closed the book and fixed her face into a smile. "Why don't we check the database?"

Catherine had wanted to avoid the database, where every single name was listed and computerized. She'd wanted finding Gionnocaro's name to feel romantic, almost accidental.

Scarlet touched her shoulder. Her face echoed Catherine's disappointment.

"Even if it's in October 1942 or August 1942, it'll take hours to find it without the database," Scarlet coaxed her. "But we're still here. It's still so, so cool that we're here."

Catherine perked up. "Thanks for saying that, honey."

Catherine and Scarlet followed Deb to a nearby computer. Deb adjusted the keyboard so that Catherine could do the honors herself. Slowly, so as not to make any mistakes, she typed Gionnocaro Fellini.

Immediately, the database spat out April 14, 1937.

Catherine jerked her head back in surprise. "What? No. That can't be right."

But Deb was already off to find the book from that date. She returned with it and spread it across a nearby oak table, using her gloved hands to flip the pages. Catherine met Scarlet's gaze.

"It must be a different Gionnocaro," she said. "There's just no way he came that early. My mother wasn't born till 1947, and I know she was born just a few years after my grandfather arrived. Not ten years after."

"I found him!" Deb called. If she'd heard Catherine's worries, she'd decided to ignore them. The database was always correct, at least in Deb's mind.

Scarlet stitched her brows together and led Catherine to the book. Sure enough, his name was in beautiful handwriting that evoked high society: Gionnocaro Fellini. He'd listed himself as an academic of all things. This made sense to Catherine, she supposed. In Italy, he'd had endless hours to pursue academia, to read philosophical texts, to become a great thinker. Until he'd lost his fortune and opened an Italian bakery—one of the first outside of Little Italy. It was the way he'd supported his family during that alienating time; the way he'd made his way in a cruel and dark America as the war ravaged on. It was often said that he hadn't more than two nickels to rub together at any given time. But he'd still raised Catherine's mother and aunts and uncle. He'd "made it," yet had destroyed his mental and physical health in the process.

"Wow," Scarlet breathed, her hands on her waist. "I can't believe he listed himself as an academic."

"It was rather common that immigrants had to pick up new ways of living once they arrived here," Deb said.

"There's no way to know how good his English was or if he had any contacts here at all."

"He went on to have an Italian bakery. It was one of the first Italian bakeries that succeeded outside of Little Italy, up in the Upper West Side," Catherine explained. "So I imagine his academic contacts were limited. He made do with family recipes. He forged his way with food."

"Just like so many Italian immigrants," Deb said. "It was an alienating time."

"I can't even imagine," Catherine breathed, still staring at her grandfather's handwriting. "I just can't figure out why my family always said he came in 1942. Because 1937 is a good chunk before that."

"Stories get convoluted," Deb said. "Maybe he told a story to his wife, who then told another story to your mother, who then told another story to you. Details get lost along the way."

"Yes, but in a historical context, 1937 is markedly different from 1942," Catherine pointed out. "The war raged heavily for the entire world by then."

Deb raised her shoulders. "The books don't lie. They're perfect records of what happened here at Ellis Island. Whatever happened after Ellis Island is a mystery to me."

"Where's his photo?" Scarlet asked.

"Should be back here," Deb said, flipping carefully to the next page.

There he was: Gionnocaro Fellini. He was solemn and clean-cut with black hair and a black mustache and large eyes. He wore an expensive-looking hat and a jacket that put him far above the photos of the photos of the other immigrants who were also pasted onto the yellow page.

Catherine's eyes filled with tears. "Do you mind if I take a photograph?" Her voice shook.

"Just make sure you don't use a flash," Deb warned.

Catherine took several with her Canon as well as with the camera on her phone. Scarlet even snapped one, proof that this was nearly as emotional for her as it was for Catherine.

Catherine and Scarlet thanked Deb profusely and shook her hand again. They headed back through the gloomy halls and into the cleansing sunshine, where a massive line of hopeful Ellis Island visitors awaited entry. They cast jealous glances at Scarlet and Catherine.

But something tugged at Catherine's heartstrings. Something felt amiss. She just couldn't put her finger on what.

On the ferry, Catherine mentioned the date again. "The year was 1942," she said. "It has to be. That's the year the bakery was open."

"Maybe he did something else before he opened the bakery?" Scarlet suggested. "Maybe he tried to join a university. Maybe he still pursued academia."

Catherine flared her nostrils. "Okay. Let's say that's true. What happened to force my grandfather to quit academia and open a bakery?"

"He didn't have enough money?"

"Sure. Yes. That's the easy and probably best answer," Catherine said. "But maybe I can reach out to Manhattan universities. Perhaps I can find records of him working on campus. Maybe I can figure out what he studied." Catherine's heart raced at the possibility of another story. She imagined finding a photograph of Gionnocaro in the library of NYU—the very university both Scarlet and Ivy attended. *Just like their great-grandfather.*

Maybe she was getting ahead of herself. But she was overjoyed at the prospect.

Catherine and Scarlet returned to the hotel briefly around noon. Catherine wanted to make notes and contact her sister, Sally. Sally lived in Dubai with her husband, which was a good eight hours ahead of East Coast US time. But Sally often stayed up late.

Catherine sent the photo of Gionnocaro from today's trip to Ellis Island, plus the text: **Look who I found! 1937, not 1942. Weird, right?**

Sally called a few minutes later. Her voice was startlingly clear, given the distance between them.

"Cathy?" Sally sounded worried.

"Hi! Can you believe it? I saw his signature and everything! He listed himself as an academic," Catherine said, speaking too quickly. "Which is why I'm going to contact a few universities around here. Maybe they have records. Maybe—"

But Sally cut her off. "Cathy, that's not our grandfather."

Catherine felt as though she'd been smacked. "What are you talking about?"

"You have photos of Grandpa somewhere, don't you?" Sally said.

"Sure." Catherine opened her laptop and pulled up the large file she'd assembled of photos of her grandfather, all of which she planned to use for the book. The photos largely began in the mid-to-late forties. There was her mother on the day of her birth. There was her grandmother, working tirelessly at the bakery with flour all over her face. There was her grandfather, smoking his pipe in the early fifties.

Catherine's heart slammed to a halt.

Again, she brought up the photo she'd taken from Ellis Island. She compared the two men. Both had large black eyes. Both had black mustaches. But their face shapes were entirely different. The man in Ellis Island had a long, slender face, a sharp jaw, while the man in the fifties had rounder features and a kinder expression.

"Maybe he just gained weight?" Catherine whispered.

"It's not him, Cathy," her sister affirmed. "Their faces are completely different. And look. In the picture you took at Ellis Island, it lists his height as five foot eight. But Grandpa was tall, remember? Over six feet."

Catherine's mouth went dry. She needed a drink of water terribly. Slowly, she got to her feet, still gaping at the image from Ellis Island and her grandfather in the fifties. "I don't understand."

"That must be why the date is wrong," her sister said. "I mean, that's not our grandfather. Our grandfather Gionnocaro came over in 1942."

"But it makes sense that he would have listed himself as an academic," Catherine protested. "He was wealthy. He came from royalty."

"Maybe he still did," Sally said. "But it's not him."

Catherine realized she'd wanted to believe this so desperately that she'd ignored the facts right in front of her face. *I wanted a fantasy. I wanted this to be him.*

"What should I do?" Catherine asked.

"I don't know. Maybe you should go back to Ellis Island?" Sally suggested. "You're still in the city, right?"

"I'm still here." Catherine collapsed in her chair and crossed her ankles. She was deflated.

"It's okay," Sally assured her. "You knew there would be some blips during your research."

Catherine rubbed her temple. She should have known. But she was such a confident researcher. How many thousands of hours had she committed to the process? It felt bizarre she'd made such a mistake.

"You're right," Catherine said finally. "I'll just go back. Maybe there's a fascinating reason behind all of this. Maybe it'll even serve the book."

"Anything for the book," Sally said with a soft laugh. "I love and miss you, Sis."

"Right back at you, Sal."

Chapter Five

Scarlet and Catherine went out for pizza that night in Little Italy. Catherine was glum and fidgety, tearing her napkin to shreds. Scarlet remembered a time when Catherine might have asked her children to stop doing that. But Scarlet knew better than to poke and prod her mother right now. Catherine was obviously mystified. She'd come to Manhattan to secure the root truth of her grandfather's immigration—and she was let down.

"We just have to go back tomorrow and ask," Scarlet assured her, touching Catherine's hand over the table.

Catherine tried to smile, but her lips immediately fell again. "I just can't believe I saw that photo and thought, 'Of course! It's him!' I mean, I grew up knowing my grandfather. It's obvious that the man in the photo is a completely different man."

Scarlet laughed gently. "It's funny what tricks the brain plays on itself, right?" She sipped her red wine, then added, "It's like me and Owen."

Catherine tilted her head with surprise. Scarlet

understood. She very rarely brought up her ex, and her mother very rarely asked about him. It was clear she was dying with curiosity.

"I wanted to believe we were happy and in love. I wanted to believe he loved me for who I was rather than the money my family had," Scarlet said.

Catherine sighed. "Oh, honey."

"I don't want pity," Scarlet reminded her sharply. "I'm just saying. Our brain isn't always there for our own self-interests. We often trip ourselves up. This is a very brief mistake that is easily rectified with another trip to Ellis Island. I'm sure there's another boatload of Gionno-caros. Maybe Deb isn't as good at her job as she thinks she is."

Catherine stifled a laugh. "You're too good to me," she said. "And wise beyond your years."

"I'm twenty-four," Scarlet said, flipping her jet-black hair behind her shoulder. "I hope I've learned a few things along the way by now."

Their pizza was a massive vegetable-and-cheese smorgasbord that left them stuffed and eager to go for a long walk through Littly Italy and Chinatown before they returned to their hotel. They decided to watch a movie—*The Talented Mr. Ripley*—during which Catherine fell asleep.

This left Scarlet with a bit of time with her own mystery.

Scarlet tiptoed into her bedroom and got under the covers. After the deletion of the Reddit post about the "conservative hippie girls," she'd asked Reddit another few questions, begging Nantucketers or anyone who vacationed there for answers. She'd gotten another ping.

> evman12: I'm pretty sure they got my
> sister. She left without leaving a note, and
> my parents are beside themselves. Let
> me know if you want to meet up to talk
> more. I live in the city but can come to
> Nantucket. I want to look for her.

Scarlet shot out of bed. Adrenaline coursed through her. Immediately, she private messaged the user and said she was in the city now. She could probably meet up before she left. She'd love to hear anything he had to say about his sister.

He responded within the hour.

> evman12: Great. I work at a cinema in
> Greenwich Village. I get off around seven
> thirty tomorrow. Maybe we can meet
> there?

Scarlet appreciated that he wanted to meet in a public and crowded place first. She wrote back that she'd be there, then wrapped herself in blankets and tried to sleep. But her thoughts twisted and contorted, and she had no control. She couldn't find sleep till sometime after two. She dreamed of bonfires on a Nantucket beach. She dreamed of young women in dresses, singing fantastical songs in strange languages.

True to Catherine Copperfield form, once Scarlet was up and out of bed, Catherine had already run five miles and re-oriented her mental state. Any depression she'd felt yesterday was a thing of the past. Scarlet sipped her coffee and listened to her mother's monologue about how exciting today would be. It wasn't till fifteen minutes in that Scarlet remembered to tell her she had plans tonight.

"It's a guy I knew at NYU." She lied because she didn't want to get into it.

Catherine looked on the verge of gushing with joy. She clasped her hands and inhaled. "That's wonderful, honey. I'm so glad."

"It's not a date," Scarlet said.

But Catherine's eyes glowed. It was as though she hadn't heard.

She just wants me to be happy, Scarlet reminded herself. She didn't want to be irritated.

Like yesterday, Scarlet and Catherine took the ferry to Ellis Island. But this time, they didn't have an appointment. They got in line and waited forty-five minutes before they were allowed inside. Far down the hallway, they spotted the blond flash of Deb's bob and hurried toward her. She gave them a curious smile.

"There seems to be a problem," Catherine explained. "That wasn't my grandfather yesterday."

Together with Deb, they returned to the database to look for all manner of Gionnocaro Fellinis. They searched for mispellings; they searched for nicknames; they searched and searched through 1942. But nothing came up.

Catherine's face was gray with dismay. Scarlet laced her fingers through her mother's and squeezed.

"I'm sorry about this," Deb said, as though the database's failure was her own. "I don't understand it. Every single name should be listed here."

Catherine sucked in her cheeks.

"Something must have happened," Deb said. "Maybe he slipped through the cracks. Like you said, he was wealthy when he arrived. Maybe he was able to pay his way into the country instead."

Catherine's eyes shifted dreamily. "Yes. That's a great point."

"I'd check libraries and record offices, things like that," Deb continued, snapping the pair of gloves she carried in her hands. "Did he live in New York for the rest of his life?"

"He did," Catherine said.

"An obituary might have more information," Deb suggested. "Leave no stone unturned."

Catherine smiled. "I worked as a journalist for many years."

"Then you already know," Deb answered.

Catherine and Scarlet left Ellis Island for the last time. Scarlet watched Catherine's face for signs of an approaching breakdown, but Catherine's jaw was firm, and she looked driven and secure.

"I'm headed for the library," Catherine said as they got off the ferry.

"I'm happy to help," Scarlet said. "I just have that meeting later."

Catherine turned to look Scarlet in the eye. Her face was difficult to read. Scarlet had the sensation she was speaking to Journalist Catherine rather than her mother.

"Why don't we meet up later?" Catherine suggested.

Scarlet understood that her mother needed space to consider what might have happened to her grandfather. She needed to pore over documents, make notes, and restructure her novel.

Scarlet didn't want to get in the way of her mother's creative and research processes.

"Sounds good," Scarlet said. "I needed a day in the city to myself anyway."

"That's my girl," Catherine said.

They hugged and parted ways. Catherine slipped into a yellow cab and waved as it bucked from the sidewalk. Scarlet had a strange and exhilarating sensation. The city spread out before her like an elaborate quilt. She had many hours until her meeting with the Reddit guy at the cinema in Greenwich Village. What could she do with her time?

Scarlet did what all New Yorkers loved most—she walked for over an hour, then sat at one of her favorite diners with a grilled cheese sandwich and a book. The book was *The Vet's Daughter* by Barbara Comyns, and it shattered her. The writing was sensational. Did people write like this anymore? She decided it was a lost art.

With still a few more hours to kill before her meeting with the Reddit guy, Scarlet checked online to see what was playing at the Greenwich Village cinema where he worked. Her idea was simple. She'd go, stake it out, maybe figure out which guy was the one she planned to meet, and figure out if he was safe. Maybe she'd even watch a movie. They were playing a few classic ones, including *Rear Window* and *All About Eve*. She decided to grab a seat for *Rear Window*. It was an Alfred Hitchcock film she'd never seen before.

Scarlet entered the cinema a few minutes after five.

"Scarlet? Scarlet Copperfield?" a voice rang out from behind the concessions counter.

Scarlet hurried forward to find Nathan Ratcliffe smiling at her. Her soul flew out of her body. Despite the silly red-and-yellow concessions hat they made him wear and a collared shirt that read GREENWICH CINEMA, he was still wonderfully handsome, with curly brown hair and big, soft, kind eyes. The eyes of a golden retriever. He was a little over six feet, with large hands and broad shoulders.

He was the first boy she'd ever kissed. Scarlet would never forget.

"Nathan?" Scarlet cried. "What are you doing here!"

Nathan walked around the concessions counter and scooped her into a hug. Scarlet inhaled his scent, which was buttery popcorn and the same cologne he'd worn back in early high school. Memories consumed her. She couldn't remember the last time she'd seen him. Probably long before she'd fallen for Owen.

"I work here," Nathan answered finally as their hug broke. "And you? I heard you skipped town."

Scarlet nodded. "I did. I left, then came back to graduate from NYU, then left again. But I'm back for a visit with my mom."

"The epic journalist," Nathan said.

"She's on the hunt for her newest story," Scarlet said. "She sent me away, though. I think I distracted her."

Nathan laughed appreciatively. "Are you here to watch a movie?"

"That was the plan. *Rear Window.*"

"It's killer," Nathan said, then laughed. "Sorry. That was a bad joke."

Scarlet shivered and smiled.

"Let me get you some popcorn," he insisted. "Any candy?"

"I'm not fourteen anymore," Scarlet said. "I can't eat everything that isn't nailed down."

Nathan laughed and patted his stomach, which was just as slender as ever. "I've gained five pounds working here," he explained.

Scarlet placed her elbows on the glass counter and

watched him prepare the popcorn, pouring melted butter over the top and shaking it. Did he know the guy from Reddit? There was a door near the popcorn machine. Maybe that led to the back offices. Perhaps that was where the Reddit guy was.

She'd know at seven thirty.

Nathan poured her a big Diet Coke and waved his hand to say she owed nothing. "Please. Soda and popcorn cost the theater nothing."

Scarlet laughed and thanked him, then paid for her ticket and walked into the dark cinema. It was nice and cool inside, like a cave, and she sat directly in the middle with the best view of the screen. Only three other people milled in. It was too early for people who worked nine-to-fives, and it wasn't exactly a hot ticket. It had been out since the fifties.

Scarlet tried to get the Reddit user and the conservative hippie-dressed girls out of her mind. For the first few minutes of the film, that proved difficult. She was hungry to tell this story; hungry to get to the bottom of it.

But then, it was as though Alfred Hitchcock performed a magic trick.

Suddenly, Scarlet was immersed in his world. Jimmy Stewart was an incredible and captivating actor. Latched away in his apartment and unable to walk, he peered out the window of his apartment, trying to make sense of what was happening in the apartment across the way. The woman who loved him—the gorgeous Grace Kelly— did everything for him, and still, it was as though Jimmy Stewart was too obsessed with his neighbor to care about her love. *That's the same as ever,* Scarlet thought to herself as she chewed her popcorn. *Men do whatever men want to do, and women try and try and try to understand them.*

But all at once, Scarlet realized she wasn't alone in her row. A man in a red-and-yellow hat sat down beside her, smelling like early high school and buttered popcorn. Scarlet's throat swelled. She glanced over and smiled at Nathan. *Why is my heart pounding so hard?*

"Who's watching the popcorn stand?" she whispered.

"My coworker has it," Nathan explained.

The Reddit guy! she thought.

Scarlet shifted her popcorn bag over to share with Nathan. He took some in his mouth but chewed so softly that she didn't hear him. It was an art form, maybe. That, or he thought of the cinema as similar to being in church.

Now that Scarlet thought about it, she wasn't sure what Nathan had done after high school. She hadn't kept track of him. He'd always been brilliant and funny and creative. It seemed bizarre that he spent his days hunkered in the shadows of a movie theater, pouring butter on popcorn. Then again, in this economy, plenty of people in the city had to work multiple jobs to pay 2500 dollars in monthly rent—and that was often just for a single room or a tiny studio.

How does anyone live? Scarlet thought.

With shame, she remembered her great-grandpa Gionnocaro and the loss of his remarkable sums of money. Had someone stolen from him when he reached America? Had he floundered it? Was that why he'd started the bakery?

What if Scarlet lost everything? Would she know how to start over from the ground up? Would she work at a cinema and make minimum wage and give herself over to the pursuit of the dollar?

Scarlet was suddenly ashamed that Nathan had to work so hard.

Then again, Scarlet had refused her father's money when she rented the apartment in the Historic District of Nantucket. She'd wanted to step out on her own for the first time. She'd wanted to know, in her heart of hearts, that she could.

The movie finished, and Nathan and Scarlet waited until the credits were finished before they stood and went into the lobby. Scarlet had a thousand things to say about the film. "I thought it was extraordinary," she said when Nathan asked.

Nathan's eyes were illuminated. He looked even more handsome when he was excited about something.

"We should talk about it sometime," Nathan said. "Maybe we could go for a drink before you go back home."

Scarlet's head spun. She would have liked to join him now. But of course, she had plans with Reddit guy. She scanned the crowd at the concessions stand, hunting for another guy dressed in a red-and-yellow hat. There was just the guy behind the counter, pimply with red hair that hung over his ears. *That must be him.* But already it was seven thirty-five, and he gave no indication of stopping.

"I wish I could take you now," Nathan confessed. "But I have plans tonight."

"Don't worry. I'm meeting someone, too," Scarlet said.

Nathan looked deflated, as though she'd just confessed to being in love with someone.

"I don't know him," Scarlet said hurriedly, then realized it sounded like she was meeting a guy from a dating app. "I mean, it's complicated."

"You don't have to explain anything to me," Nathan assured her. "We haven't seen each other in years."

"It doesn't seem that long right now," Scarlet confessed. She couldn't believe she was so honest.

Together, Nathan and Scarlet stood in silence in the lobby of the theater. Scarlet's eyes went left to right, left to right. Still, there was no sign of the pimply worker hanging up his apron and leaving for the day.

"You can go," Nathan told her. "I'm still waiting for someone."

Scarlet felt the words like electricity through her body. "You're waiting for someone? Here?"

Nathan's lips twisted into a funny smile. "Don't tell me you're on Reddit."

Scarlet's mouth hung open. A beat of silence came between them. And then, she felt only horror. She took his elbow and said, "Maddie's gone."

Nathan dropped his head forward and stared at his shoes. The look on his face was all the information she needed. *Maddie joined the group on Nantucket. But why?*

"Let's get that drink right now," Scarlet said softly. "It looks like you need it."

"More than anything," Nathan said. His eyes were soft and round.

Chapter Six

Catherine stood in front of the New York Public Library with her heart in her throat. Two mighty stone lions guarded the entrance, and a strangely chilly breeze cut through the trees of Central Park and reminded her that autumn would soon sweep the summer air away and cleanse everything. Before she went inside, she watched a young mother walk hand in hand with two little girls with black hair. They might have been Ivy and Scarlet, deliriously happy with the books they'd selected and ready to read them again and again in the park.

I don't understand time. Where does it go? Catherine thought.

Her grandfather must have felt the same when the war pushed him out of Europe. War was the most nonsensical thing. Yet it was as old as humankind.

Inside the library, Catherine made her way to the records office and asked to go through the numerous New York City newspapers. She wanted to look at Gionnocaro's obituary first. She wanted to read about her grandfather, about the man she'd always known.

It didn't take long for Catherine to find her grandfather's obituary.

Gionnocaro Fellini (1921-1994) was born in Rome, Italy, to a royal family, yet lost everything when he came to America in 1942. Remembering his country's remarkable baking traditions, he founded the first Italian bakery in the Upper East Side. Despite a difficult start, the bakery was always known for giving out free bread to the struggling families in the area and generally promoting goodwill during the city's most difficult times. He went on to marry the beautiful Gwen in 1945, and they welcomed their first daughter, Vivian, in 1947, followed by two more daughters (Val and Nadine) and a son (Jack). By the sixties, the bakery was one of the most talked about sights in the Upper East Side, although Gionnocaro liked to joke that baking only ever lent a margin of the wealth he'd once enjoyed back in Italy. Gionnocaro never returned to Italy, but he adored his city, his family, and later, his grandchildren (Catherine, Sally, Patty, Jefferson, Matthew, Addison, Bert, and Walt).

The photo attached to the obituary was of the man Catherine had once adored and loved. Her heart ached to see him—just a little bit younger than he'd been when she was a girl, with Coke-bottle glasses and a mischievous grin.

Catherine had never known her grandma Gwen. But Gionnocaro had always spoken of Gwen with a look that told just how much he still adored her, even in death.

Catherine sat back in her chair and crossed her arms over her chest. Across the room were other people, peering down through microscopes to read the fine print of ancient newspapers. The newspapers themselves were protected and archived. It felt as though they were Indiana Jones–types diving back through history.

Now, Catherine wanted to figure out who the other Gionnocaro Fellini was. Maybe it was a dead end. Perhaps it had nothing to do with her. But something about the fact that he was the *only* Gionnocaro Fellini in Ellis Island records intrigued her.

It doesn't make any sense.

Catherine searched through the archives to discover any news of Gionnocaro Fellini from 1937, 1938, and 1939.

Finding the first mention of the "intellectual" Gionnocaro Fellini didn't take long.

It was in a newspaper clipping from October 17, 1938—just a year and a half after his arrival.

Newly arrived Gionncaro Fellini is a PhD in residence at New York University. His studies in the field of linguistics focus on the link between Germanic and romantic languages. Here he is photographed at his recent wedding to another intellectual and female student at NYU, Dee Philips Fellini.

Catherine peered at the photo for a good twenty-five minutes. In it, the other Gionnocaro and his new wife,

Dee, were unsmiling, photographed arm in arm in front of a Manhattan church that Catherine had probably passed by thousands of times. Dee was beautiful, wearing a practical wedding dress from the late thirties. Her cheeks were hollow, and she didn't look particularly happy—perhaps because it was so difficult to be an accepted female academic back in those days.

Catherine hoped Gionnocaro had respected Dee. It was clear he thought she was smart, at least. Otherwise, he would have married someone who wasn't studying at NYU.

Other people were in the photograph as well. Beautifully dressed people, all of whom probably knew they were headed for war. Europe was already raging. Catherine studied their faces, the frilly dresses, the hats.

A face toward the right-hand side of the photograph caught her attention. Her spine straightened.

She looks just like me.

Catherine gaped at the very young woman. Her face was turned so that she looked at the bride and groom. She wore a dark dress and a black hat and carried a bouquet. Had that been Dee's bouquet? The young woman might have been seventeen or eighteen. She was unnamed. But she really did have Catherine's and Scarlet's and Ivy's and Sally's features. She might have been a lost relative.

Catherine was suddenly consumed with the need to read as much as she could about Dee and Gionnocaro.

Maybe she could figure out who the young woman was. Perhaps she was a sister or a cousin. Maybe she was an employee.

Hours passed. Catherine flew through the archives, reading about Gionnocaro's discoveries in the field of linguistics, about Dee's graduation, about the arrival of their first child—a boy named Stephan Fellini. Clearly, this Gionnocaro still had his wealth, and he liked to flaunt it with dinners out and ballroom dances and meet and greets with the elite in Hollywood at the time. He photographed well and seemed only to get more handsome as time passed. Dee seemed increasingly haggard, and Catherine could only speculate what the trouble was. Maybe Gionnocaro was having affairs. Perhaps he was spending their money too quickly. Maybe she was struggling with being a mother and a student at the same time. Presumably they had help, but there was often too much pressure on a mother's shoulders no matter what.

It wasn't till the library announced its closure that Catherine discovered one more clue about the woman.

There was a photograph taken in 1941. In it were Gionnocaro, Dee, baby Stephan, baby Francine, and that woman from the wedding. Again, this woman had Catherine's face. Catherine's heart pounded. *Who are you?*

The caption read: **Gionnocaro, Dee, and their children, Stephan and baby Francine, vacation in the Hamptons. To the right is their nanny, Gwen.**

Catherine's heart stopped. *Gwen? Grandma Gwen?* She gaped at the image and crossed her arms so tightly she thought she might break her ribs.

Suddenly, a library staff member appeared at her desk and demanded she leave for the night. Catherine took another few photographs and put everything away. She then shot into the darkening night with tears in her eyes.

If that's really my grandma Gwen, she worked for

Gionnocaro Fellini—a man with wealth and prosperity here in New York City.

She worked for him before my grandfather ever arrived.

What did it mean? Catherine couldn't get her head around it. But something smelled off.

Chapter Seven

Nathan led Scarlet to a little dive bar in Greenwich Village called Johnny's. An ancient jukebox was at the bar's far end, and stools lined a long bar counter. There was very little space for anything else. It was still early—just a few minutes before eight—and only a few others nursed their beers in peace. The real crowd would come in sometime after nine thirty and liven the place up.

"Howdy, Nathan," the bartender said, rapping his knuckles on the bar top. "Been a couple of weeks. How're things?"

"All good," Nathan said, then stuttered, "This is an old friend of mine. Scarlet."

"Any friend of Nathan's is a friend of mine," the bartender said. "What can I get for ya?"

Scarlet ordered a glass of white wine—something simple to calm her jitters—and Nathan went for a dark beer. They sat toward the far end of the bar, nearest the jukebox. Neither of them knew what to say.

It was terribly bizarre that they'd reconnected on

Reddit. But, Scarlet supposed, stranger things had happened. They were happening all the time. *Like this "cult" or whatever it is.*

"So," Scarlet said, unsure of her voice. "What does 'evman12' mean?"

"What's that?"

"Your Reddit username."

Nathan wrinkled his nose and let out an exhausted laugh. "Oh. I came up with that like ten years ago. I forget what it means. I think it has something to do with a movie I was into at the time." He laughed again. "You know better than to bring up someone's online presence."

"You're right. It was rude of me." Scarlet filled her mouth with wine. "I'm really sorry to hear about Maddie."

Nathan's smile fell. "Yeah."

"She was Ivy's age, right?"

"Yes. She was supposed to start her sophomore year at Columbia this September," he said. "But she disappeared in March or April."

"Without a trace?"

"Not exactly," he said. "Sometimes my parents hear from her. She asks for money. They're terrified and want to give her whatever she needs, so they send it. I mean, she's only nineteen years old."

"Have they contacted the police?"

"Yes. That's the first thing they did. But the police can't do anything if she left on her own. On purpose."

"What makes you think she's involved in this crew on Nantucket?" Scarlet asked. Slowly, she removed a notepad from her backpack and began to write down what Nathan told her. Any tiny clue could lead to something. She'd learned this from her father.

"Because she came home exactly one time," Nathan said. "And I happened to be there."

Scarlet gaped at him. Her pen was frozen over her notepad.

"She knew my parents were out," Nathan said. "It was a big gala event they always attended every year that demanded thousands and thousands of dollars per ticket. I don't live at home anymore, obviously. Ever since I went to film school, my dad and I haven't exactly seen eye to eye. But I was there, looking for an old DVD of *Taxi Driver* I'd bought back in high school. I heard someone come into the apartment. You remember where I lived, right? It was an apartment building like yours. The doorman wouldn't have let her in if he didn't recognize her. Anyway, I assumed it was my parents or something. But the person crept around like they were trying to rob the place. I got freaked out. I grabbed a baseball bat from my old bedroom and tiptoed through the halls until I reached Maddie's old room. There she was, crouched on the floor, rummaging through an old shoebox. There was a load of cash to the right of it. I'm guessing it was cash she'd gotten from graduation or something. I don't know. My parents weren't always keen on putting every bit of cash into the bank. It was an old family rule. *Trust no one.*

"Finally, Maddie noticed my presence and turned to look at me. Her eyes were feral. That's when I realized what she was wearing. A super long skirt. A blouse that made her look super hippie-dippy. And her hair was crazy long and scraggly."

"When was this?" Scarlet asked. Her voice was hardly a whisper.

"The gala's always at the end of June. Must have been around then," he said.

"What did you say to her?"

"I mean, I'm her older brother. This is my kid sister we're talking about. So I leaned against the doorway and tried to tease her. I was like, 'You're in big trouble, you know?' She jumped up and scooped all the money into her arms. She looked at me as though I were a monster she'd been warned about. I didn't understand it because we'd always had a great relationship.

"I changed tactics after that. I asked, 'What are you wearing? What kind of people are you hanging out with? Are you Amish or something?' She got really nasty and said, 'You've bought into all their propaganda. You're a sheep.' And then she tore past me, grabbed a tote bag, and stuffed all the money inside. I ran after her, but she was always quick, and I was always clumsy. She got the elevator before me. I got the next one. But when I reached the foyer downstairs, the doorman said she'd already gotten into a taxi and left. He looked just as freaked out as me. He said, 'That was my Maddie! I've known her since she was a baby girl! How could I say no to her?' I felt bad after that. My parents were really angry with the doorman. They wanted to have him fired for not keeping Maddie back. But luckily, they were able to just move him to another building rather than fire him."

Scarlet shook her head. Little Maddie! She remembered her just as the doorman

did. Bright and happy and silly and free.

"One of the girls I saw in Nantucket was one of Ivy's classmates, too," Scarlet explained.

"Do you think they're all girls from rich families in Manhattan?" Nathan asked.

"It's certainly possible. It's easy for them to call their parents and ask for money," Scarlet said. "But it means someone is at the top of all of this. Someone is manipulating them."

"Someone who thinks he's a Charles Manson type," Nathan said. His eyes were stormy. He drank too much of his beer at once and wiped his mouth with the back of his hand.

Scarlet understood. If Ivy were involved in something like this, she'd be heartbroken, but she'd also be deliriously angry.

"I didn't know their base could be Nantucket till I read your post," Nathan said. "I thought about coming out there immediately. But funds are tight for me at the moment. I cut myself off from my family, which was probably stupid. And I make ends meet with the cinema and a few other odd jobs."

"I guess they didn't want you to go to film school?"

"It doesn't sit right with my dad that I don't want to go into finance like him," Nathan said. "He can't understand what he did wrong. But my parents are both distracted and despondent now. They want Maddie back. She was their golden child who always did everything right." Nathan sighed. "It doesn't matter what my parents think of me. But I love my little sister. I don't want her involved in this. And I certainly don't want some egomaniac manipulating her to get to my family's money. I didn't refuse it just for some guy to fund his cult with it."

Scarlet continued to scribble notes to herself on her notepad. Nathan watched for a moment and then ordered them another round of drinks. Unbeknownst to Scarlet, nearly an hour had passed.

Scarlet set down her pen and took another sip of wine. Her head throbbed.

"I want to get to the bottom of this," she told him. "The plan was to make a documentary about it and discover the truth as I dug deeper. But I understand if that's too sensitive. If you want me to stop pursuing it, it's all right."

"No," Nathan said in a formidable tone. "I'd like to help you. If you want that."

Scarlet swallowed the lump in her throat. Desperation glimmered behind his eyes.

Nathan said, "I went to film school. I studied documentaries and feature films, sound and design, and art and writing. I went as far as I possibly could on a student level, and then, I mostly gave up because I hate LA and can't afford to make movies here. But this? Something so personal? It's what I've been waiting for."

Scarlet's stomach began to hurt. *If he joins me, it means it isn't fully mine anymore. But it matters to him. And the story will come alive with his involvement.*

It means I won't be able to back out when it gets hard.

"Tell me what I should do," Nathan said, raising his chin.

"Can you take some time off your jobs?"

Nathan snorted. "Probably not."

Scarlet lowered her eyes. They had to be in Nantucket for the documentary to work.

"But I can quit," Nathan said.

Scarlet's laughter caught in her throat. "Are you sure?"

"I think I can get another few crappy jobs when I get back to the city," he said. "I'm not worried about that. I am worried about my sister. I'm worried about my parents, safe in their ivory tower, their hearts breaking more and more by the minute. And you know they're not the only ones. These parents aren't all talking to each other. They're embarrassed that their children ran away and refuse to pool their efforts to fix this. Again, because they're embarrassed. This type of thing happens to other people. Not them." Nathan sipped his beer. "You know how the Manhattan elite are."

Scarlet raised her eyebrows and continued to write. "Oh, I do. I really do." She raised her chin to look at him. She enjoyed a flashing image of a memory: his lips upon hers; their bodies not knowing what to do; their lips loose and confused. It had probably been a terrible kiss, but it had been their first, which made it special.

"Would you mind if I interview you properly for the documentary?" she asked. "We could set you up some-where, maybe on a Nantucket beach."

"Of course not," he said. "I'd just tell the camera everything I just told you."

"Perfect," Scarlet said.

Another moment of silence passed between them. Scarlet felt so strange, almost as though she were dream-ing. She reached for Nathan's hand, and he let her hold it for a few seconds before he pulled away. Maybe the inti-macy was too intense for him. Or perhaps he had a girl-friend he hadn't told her about.

Scarlet tried to wade around that to get an answer.

"Is it going to be difficult for you to leave the city?" she asked.

"Like I said, I'll quit my jobs and sublet my room."

"But I mean, are any people going to miss you here?" Scarlet asked, sounding tentative.

Nathan's eyes widened when it clicked. "I just went

through a breakup in late spring, around the time Maddie disappeared."

"I'm sorry." Scarlet's heart swelled.

"It's okay. We weren't right for each other," Nathan assured her.

"Is anyone right for each other?" Scarlet asked with a laugh.

"I don't know. Our parents are still together," Nathan pointed out. His mischievous smile returned for a split second, then disappeared into his scowl again.

"True. It feels like a fluke," Scarlet said. "But I know it took decades and decades of hard work. And I know my mother's career always went on the back burner."

"You think she resents him?" Nathan asked.

"I ask myself that all the time," Scarlet admitted. "She's very good at loving my father. She's very good at loving us. But after her cancer—"

Nathan's face broke. Both hands swept to the sides of his face. "I completely forgot. I should have said something immediately."

Scarlet's heart warmed. "No. It's okay. She's okay."

"I heard it was a tough time," Nathan said. "Your family left not long after that?"

"She had surgery, Dad quit his job, and we all bounced to Nantucket," Scarlet said. "I left NYU for a brief time, too. It was topsy-turvy."

"Sounds like it."

Scarlet thought Nathan had the unique capability of listening, asking questions, and staying interested in what she said. It was far different from any man she'd ever gone out with. What made him so empathetic? Was it his interest in film?

"I still can't believe we ran into each other like this," Scarlet said. "It feels like fate."

"I don't believe in fate," Nathan said with a slow smile.

"What do you believe in?"

Nathan pulled off his concession stand hat, folded it, and shoved it in his back pocket. "I believe in quitting bad jobs. I believe in moving on. And I believe we're going to find my sister and whoever's behind this. We have to."

Scarlet squeezed his hand. "We have to."

Chapter Eight

Catherine's mother, Vivian, was born in 1947—five years after Catherine's grandfather immigrated to the United States. She lived in California with her tabby cat, Princess, down the street from Catherine's cousin Walt, who often checked in on her. She was seventy-seven years old but just as intellectually spry as ever.

Vivian answered on the second ring. Catherine walked the exterior of Central Park as daylight dimmed over the city and streetlamps flickered on. She planned to walk back to the hotel and then research whatever she could online.

But she also wanted to dig around her mother's memories for answers.

"How's my darling daughter?" Vivian asked.

"Great, Mom. I'm in the city," Catherine said.

"You're back! I can't imagine why you ever left. Nantucket's beautiful for a few months out of the year, but don't you miss the culture? The life? The restaurants?

I've lost my mind looking at the ocean all these years. It's just too big. My thoughts get lost."

"You're the one who left New York forty years ago," Catherine pointed out.

"You know UCLA was the only university that would support my research."

Catherine smiled into the phone. It pleased her that her mother was such a whip-smart lady; that she'd given so much of her life and her effort to the pursuit of knowledge in scientific research, alongside being a mother and a wife. Her field had been ecology. She'd studied bird routes from Canada to Brazil and given several early-year Ted Talks about the environment. *My mother is smarter than me,* Catherine had told Quentin early on. Quentin had insisted it wasn't true until he'd met Vivian. And then he'd said, *You're equals. It's terrifying.*

"You're out for a walk, aren't you?" Vivian asked. "I can hear all the horns screaming. It's making me nostalgic."

"I'm not far from where you grew up," Catherine said.

"Oh! I so loved the city in the summer," Vivian said. "Especially in August. Everyone left for the Hamptons. It was divine to have the city to ourselves."

Catherine listened to her mother talk about the past and her childhood for a few minutes. Her heart swelled with love for her.

"Did you ever go down to Little Italy and hang with the other Italian children?" Catherine asked after a while. She couldn't believe she'd never asked it before.

"It was so far away," Vivian admitted. "We tended to stick with the other families in the Upper East Side, and most of them weren't Italian. There were loads of kids around and so much trouble to get into. My father and mother always chased us out of the bakery."

Gwen.

"I wanted to ask you," Catherine said. "Do you know what your mother was up to before Grandpa got to America?" She wet her lips, trying to keep her tone light. She hadn't told her mother about her idea for the book yet. She hadn't been sure how to pitch it.

In a way, Vivian was a much more difficult audience to please than even Greta Copperfield.

"My mother was raised in New York," Vivian said. "But she was really quite secretive about her past. She died too young for me to get a real grip on it. I was young and selfish myself. I didn't know what questions to ask before it was too late. I didn't know what I would want to know."

"Did you ask your father before he passed?"

"No," Vivian said. "But you remember how he was. He had so many stories himself from the old country. He couldn't get enough of telling them. All that wealth they had! Those gorgeous castles! It all sounded so mesmerizing to me as a child. I always imagined that Mother was raised in some Manhattan slums. It sounded too sad to me, especially when I could return to Father's stories."

Catherine paused at a crosswalk and waited for the red to turn green. "I've been wondering," she said tentatively, "how was it that Grandpa lost his money? Had he already lost it when he got to America? Or did he lose it once he got here?"

"Haven't I told you the story?" Vivian asked.

"No! I would have remembered it." Catherine had searched her mind for any hint but found nothing.

"Goodness. Well, you remember what a funny guy

your grandfather was. He was impatient and rash and all over the place. His moods were just as all over the place. Happy one minute; sad the next; frantic the next. My poor mother was the only woman who knew how to handle him. In any case, he always said he got onboard that ship *to go to America,* and immediately got so painfully homesick and frightened and goshdarn bored that he had to do something with his time. Something to distract himself. So he set up a poker game with some of the guys on board. Some were wealthy; others were not.

"Your grandfather was notoriously bad at poker," Vivian said. "He was also something of a gambling addict. That first night, he was up twenty-thousand dollars, or so he said. And after that, he proceeded to lose all of it."

"All of it?" Catherine could hardly believe it.

"It took three weeks to get to America," Vivian said. "My father always described that period as his metamorphosis. He boarded a rich man, and he left the ship a very poor man."

"Huh."

"It's a fascinating story," Vivian said. It was clear she'd never probed deeper into it. She'd taken it at face value.

Because her father told her that story. And she believed her father above everyone else.

It was romantic to believe the ones you loved.

Maybe it's still true, Catherine thought. But she was beginning to see the cracks in his tale.

"What did he come to America to do?" Catherine asked.

Vivian sounded huffy. "You know he had to escape the war. He didn't want to fight for Italy and the Germans, and he wanted to pursue his academics in the New World."

"But he didn't pursue academia," Catherine pointed out. *The other Gionnocaro did.*

"He had to make money as quickly as he could," Vivian said. "I believe he answered an ad in the paper for a little place in the Upper East Side and set up his bakery by the end of that first year, 1942. After that, he was consumed by the bakery. As was my mother."

Catherine had reached her hotel. She entered the lobby and smiled at the receptionist. She wanted to get on the elevator, but she didn't want to lose her mother. So she hung around the shadowy hotel bar for a few minutes to wrap up the conversation. She felt she hadn't gotten much out of it. *Just more lies, maybe.*

"Is it possible that Grandma Gwen used to work as a nanny for wealthy families?" Catherine asked.

"It's certainly possible," Vivian said. She sounded like she didn't care.

"And she never mentioned any wealthy families she might have worked for?"

"Where is all this coming from?" Vivian demanded.

But Catherine didn't have enough information to explain everything yet, and she didn't want to distract her mother so soon before she went to bed that night. It was nearly ten here, which made it seven in LA. Her mother liked her beauty rest. She resented anyone who upset her.

"Do you have any old photographs of Grandma Gwen from the late thirties? Before she met Grandpa?" Catherine asked, then bit her tongue.

"I do. Somewhere."

"Would you mind taking pictures of them and sending them to me?" Catherine asked.

"Should I scan them?" Vivian suggested.

"No, no. Just use your phone to take photos of them as best as you can," Catherine said, praying that her mother would use natural light.

Catherine never liked explaining new technology to her mother. She always felt like technology was going too quickly for even herself. She hated how it made her mother feel small and obsolete. Catherine would probably feel like that soon, too.

"I'll do it as soon as we get off the phone," Vivian promised.

"Thank you. I love you, Mom."

"And I love you, too, honey." Vivian was quiet for a moment. "I hope you'll ask me everything you want to know before I go."

Catherine's heart seized with worry. She hated when her mother referred to her own death.

"I'll pepper you with endless questions next time I see you," Catherine said.

"This has been a good start," Vivian said. Catherine could hear the smile in her voice.

Chapter Nine

Scarlet returned to the hotel by eleven thirty that night. She felt buzzy and adrenalized and unsure how she would account for all her time away to her mother. But her mother's door was already closed. She'd left a note on the table in the main room that said, "Pretty beat. Love you. See you in the morning."

Scarlet tried to parse the meaning behind the note. What had happened at the library? Had her mother discovered more about her great-grandfather Gionnocaro?

Of course, Scarlet understood how her mother got when she was immersed in a project. It was as though the rest of the world filtered away and left only the bare bones of what she needed to know and what she wanted to learn.

Scarlet showered the beer smell of Johnny's Bar off and got into bed. It was hard to believe the day she'd had. It was exhilararting to remember every beat; she never wanted to forget it. The fact that Nathan had turned out to be her Reddit poster; that they'd watched the film together; that they'd laughed and cried together at the bar felt like too much.

Now, Nathan had promised to quit his multiple jobs and give up his apartment and come to Nantucket to break the story.

But that was unlikely to happen. Wasn't it?

Because Scarlet couldn't sleep, she decided to call Ivy to see what was up at home. Ivy didn't answer but sent a text that read: **What's up? I'm out.** It was succinct and cool.

> SCARLET: It's been super weird in NYC. Wanted to chat.

> IVY: You come back tomorrow? I'll see you then.

Scarlet knew Ivy was out with her secret boyfriend. She threw her phone to the foot of her bed, just as it buzzed with another message. Scarlet told herself to let it be. But curiosity eventually got to her, and she whipped up to read it.

> NATHAN: It was so good to see you.

The words sent electricity through her arms and down her body, all the way to her toes. She fell back against the pillows and stared at his name. Something about him attracted her more than she could really say. Was it the fact that he'd rejected his parents' money to make it on his own? Was it because he loved art and film and music so much? Or was it just this intense attraction between them—one that seemed chemical?

She didn't know. And she wasn't sure she'd ever find out.

It would be crazy if Nathan really came to Nantucket. He would surely drop out.

* * *

The following morning, Scarlet got up early and read over her notes from her night with Nathan, making adjustments here and there and visualizing the interview itself. Maybe, if Nathan didn't agree to come to Nantucket, she could still come back to NYC and interview him in front of a green screen or something. Maybe he'd still agree to be minorly involved.

Catherine returned from her run at seven. Scarlet was in the main room, drinking coffee and nibbling peanuts she happened to have in her bag. A light hangover spread through the back of her skull. She needed an egg-bacon-cheese sandwich from a bodega. She needed something greasy or fried.

Catherine looked frantic. She sat on the floor to stretch. Her breathing was ragged.

"How was your day?" Scarlet finally asked.

"Huh?" Catherine looked up. It was almost as though she was surprised to see Scarlet there.

"How was the library?" Scarlet asked again.

"Oh! It was fine."

This was startlingly low on information. "Did you find more stuff about Great-Grandpa?"

"A little bit," Catherine admitted. "I want to go back today."

Scarlet bowed her head. When her mother had asked her to come to Manhattan, Scarlet had imagined helping her; digging through the archives together; discovering secrets about their family. But Catherine was being cagey.

"Do you mind?" Catherine asked, her voice brightening. "I mean, I know you have your own things to take care of. Your own friends and projects."

She said it with hope in her voice. Scarlet still refused to tell her mother anything about her project. Not until she knew more. Not until she'd fleshed it out herself.

Once, Catherine had confessed that she was the same way with her own mother. That Vivian was so intellectual and authoritative and *terrifying* that Catherine liked to keep things close to her chest until she knew exactly how to articulate them.

Scarlet knew that Catherine would be brokenhearted if she knew Scarlet thought the same way about her as she did about Vivian. But life was cyclical like that.

Catherine showered and left an hour later. Scarlet pulled on her tennis shoes and left not long after that, stepping breezily through the streets until she found a bodega with a perfect breakfast sandwich and burnt coffee. She sat on a picnic table outside and people-watched for a while. It was a little too hot to sit like that, totally exposed to the elements, and the people who passed in their business clothing were sweating and often angry.

Suddenly, she longed for Nantucket.

A text came through from Nathan.

NATHAN: Hey! I just quit my jobs, and I'm about to meet with a few people who want to sublet my room. Want to hang out while they come over?

Scarlet cackled with surprise. A woman in a suit jacket gave her a terrifying look, as though her happiness wasn't wanted this early.

SCARLET: I'll be right there.

Scarlet decided to take the subway to the Lower East Side and reached Nathan's apartment by ten thirty. He buzzed her inside, and she hurried up three flights of stairs to discover Nathan in the quaint living room of a four-bedroom apartment he shared with three other people in their twenties. This was the reality of rejecting the money your parents had. There were a lot of dirty dishes in the sink.

Nathan looked happy and big-eyed, as though he'd just won a prize that had changed his entire life. He'd just made himself a big plate of eggs and greeted Scarlet with a hug. "Welcome!"

Scarlet laughed and came inside. "I can't believe you quit."

"I said I would," Nathan said with a shrug.

Scarlet's pulse quickened. *It means the documentary is real. It's happening.*

I have to fully face it, now.

I owe him.

"Were they angry?" Scarlet asked.

"What? No way. People quit those jobs all the time," Nathan said. "It's not like they offered a pension plan."

Scarlet laughed and tried to get comfortable on his sofa, but it felt like it was made of cardboard and cotton balls.

"I'm between visitors," Nathan said. "But the rent is cheap. I'm guessing one of these people will take it."

Very soon after that, a girl in her early twenties with what looked to be twelve piercings on each ear came in, took one look at the room, and said she could move in right away. The rent of nine-fifty was a sneeze for her, apparently. Scarlet sucked in her cheeks and watched as the woman sent the money to Nathan with her phone.

Nathan smacked his thighs. "Looks like I need a place to stay in Nantucket!"

"You're going to Nantucket?" the girl with the piercings asked, chewing her gum.

"We have a project there," he explained.

"My parents have a place there," the girl said.

"Everyone's parents have a place there!" Nathan threw up his hands.

"Do yours?" Scarlet asked, hoping he might be able to stay there.

"Mine are Hamptons' people," Nathan explained.

Scarlet tucked a strand of hair behind her ear. It was suddenly clear he needed to stay with her in the Historic District. There was no other way.

The girl went into her room, slammed the door, and immediately launched into a voice message in a language neither Nathan nor Scarlet understood. Scarlet wanted to get out of there.

"My mom doesn't want to leave till tomorrow or the next day," Scarlet admitted. "But I'm happy to get out of the city now."

Nathan tilted his head. "You sure?"

"She's lost in her own research," Scarlet said, waving her hand. "And it sounds like you need a bed tonight."

"Do you have a spare?" Nathan asked with a laugh, rubbing the back of his neck. "I didn't even ask. Maybe I was rash?"

"No. It's exciting. Really." Scarlet wet her lips. Adrenaline coursed through her. "You want to come back to my hotel with me? I can pack up my stuff, and then..."

"We'll take the bus."

Scarlet laughed. "I guess that's the only way."

Nathan had already packed a large hiking backpack with everything he wanted to bring, including recording and film equipment he'd brought home from film school. It was hard to gauge what else was in there. Toiletries? Underwear? It was August in Nantucket, which meant he didn't require much more than a swimsuit and a few T-shirts and shorts.

What if he stays longer? Scarlet asked herself, then immediately quieted the voice.

Nathan and Scarlet buzzed down the street. They talked quickly, exchanging exciting ideas about how they could get to the bottom of this and begin the documentary. They talked about movies they liked and documentaries they wanted to honor; they talked about the documentary film festival they wanted to be featured at.

They talked and talked and talked.

Scarlet thought they would never run out of things to say.

Once in their hotel, Scarlet tried to call her mother, but Catherine didn't answer. So she sent a text and wrote a note, then packed up and headed with Nathan for the bus station. It was a rare form of transportation for a girl of such privilege. But Nathan had once been privileged, too.

Nathan and Scarlet got on the bus and sped out of the city, back to Nantucket.

"I feel like I'm escaping a prison," Nathan said as

New York City got smaller and smaller out the window. "I think it was about to suffocate me."

"I know what you mean," Scarlet breathed.

Chapter Ten

Back at the library, Catherine hunted for her grandmother Gwen.

At first, she discovered her only in photographs taken with the rich intellectual Italian Gionnocaro Fellini's family. Gwen was situated in the background of Dee's baby shower, which was written about in the Style section of the paper. In another photo published a few years later, she held baby Stephan at Dee's next baby shower. She looked secretive and dark and beautiful. But she'd been a woman who'd come from nothing. What was her past? And how had she gotten involved with the Gionnocaro Fellini family?

How had she come to marry another Gionnocaro Fellini?

Catherine decided to backtrack. She took a deep breath.

She left the library for a half hour to grab a cup of coffee and write notes to herself. She felt as though she were chasing multiple ghosts. It was around now that Scarlet called her, then called her again. But Catherine

"

was too immersed in her note-taking to answer. It wasn't long after that that Scarlet wrote she was headed back to Nantucket. Catherine considered writing her back. But that was when she thought, *Go back to the library. Find the announcement for the bakery.*

And that was what she did.

According to the archives, her grandfather Gionnocaro married Gwen in early 1945. Despite her grandfather's supposed "royalty," there was no photograph of Gwen and Gionnocaro in the papers. Just a brief announcement.

If he was so important, why wasn't it a bigger deal that he married? Even if he'd lost everything, wasn't he known?

Why didn't he want to live with other Italians? Why did he come to the Upper East Side rather than move to Little Italy with everyone else?

Six months after Gionnocaro and Gwen's wedding, the bakery opened in the Upper East Side. There was a tiny photograph of Gwen and Gionnocaro outside the bakery, plus the description: "Once-royal Italian Gionnocaro Fellini lost it all. But he's committed to feeding the locals of the Upper East Side until the war ends and the United States enjoys peace once more."

The photograph was of her grandfather and grandmother. There was no mention of the other Gionnocaro Fellini. Wouldn't that have been a funny mention? The fact that they had the same name?

But the other Gionnocaro was still semi-royal. The other one was wealthy. The other one didn't lose it all.

Did they know each other back in Italy? Did they have some kind of rivalry?

Catherine was stumped. She leaned back in her chair

and studied the crown molding in the library. She studied the strange hair barrette of the woman across the room from her. She thought and thought and thought until another message came through from Scarlet, saying she was halfway home. On the bus, of all things.

Catherine's heart stung. *Shoot. Shoot.*

Catherine hurried outside to call Scarlet. It felt as though she emerged from a dream. Scarlet answered on the third ring. It sounded like someone was laughing nearby. A man.

Wasn't she out last night? Who was she with? Why didn't I ask?

Oh, but she's twenty-four. She can take care of herself.

"Are you all right, honey?" Catherine asked.

"Hi! I'm fine. I just realized I had some stuff to do at home," Scarlet said.

Catherine's stomach roiled. "I'm sorry. I shouldn't have left you alone like that. I mean, I invited you to come, and then I got so distracted." She bowed her head with shame.

"Don't worry about it," Scarlet ordered. "Really. It was wonderful to be back in the city."

It felt as though there was a great, shadowy distance between them.

Catherine cursed herself. *It feels like the same distance between my mother and me.*

"I'll see you when you get back," Scarlet said.

"Yes," Catherine said. "Let me know when you do. Don't work too hard."

"Love you."

"I love you, too," Catherine said. She inhaled sharply. "So much."

Catherine retreated inside and sat back down in front

of the archives. As she had many times in the past, she felt like a captive to the narrative that unfolded via her research. It consumed her.

I beat cancer. I'm still here. I'm still here to chase stories to the bitter end.

This pleased her more than anything.

Based on instinct, Catherine decided to read more about the first Gionnocaro and Dee. What had happened to them after they'd had their children and their beautiful baby showers and their gala events? How had Gionnocaro's research gone? Had he discovered anything tremendous? Had he changed the course of academia?

It wasn't long till Catherine had her answer.

It was an obituary.

Catherine's jaw hung open as she read.

Gionnocaro Fellini (1919 - 1945) was born in Rome, Italy, to Princesss Aurora Bellini and Prince Fernando Fellini. He came to the United States in 1937 to study at New York University and later went on to marry Dee Fellini and have two children, Stephan and Francine. A visitation and memorial service will be held Saturday at one p.m. at St. Matthews Cathedral.

Catherine hadn't realized she'd gotten to her feet. Again and again, she read the obituary until she got up the nerve to dig deeper. How had Gionnocaro died?

At first, it felt hopeless. The density of history was often difficult to dig through—especially eighty years later. But eventually, the week after the obituary was published, Catherine discovered an article: "Was Foul Play Involved in Italian Royal's Death?"

Catherine's heartbeat intensified. She could hardly breathe.

A horrible thought wormed its way through her mind. *Was it possible that her grandfather and grandmother had something to do with this? Was it possible they'd killed the first Gionnocaro, stolen his identity, and then started the bakery?*

Catherine read the article, which was a brief yet intense interview with the police captain at the time of Gionnocaro's death.

The officer said, "The deceased was found face-down in his study. His wife and children were in the Hamptons for the weekend. There were no wounds on his body. But with a wealthy man like this, one tends to speculate that foul play was involved. Perhaps he was poisoned."

When asked if the police captain had any evidence to back this up, the captain said only, "The wife wanted Gionnocaro buried almost immediately after his death. This didn't allow us to perform any tests or deduce the reason for death. However, it should be noted that a few staff members disappeared immediately after Gionnocaro's death. I asked Mrs. Fellini if those staff members took anything with them, anything of value. But she was unfortunately too despondent to understand what I was talking about."

Catherine sucked in her cheeks. *Staff members.* Could one of those staff members have been Gwen?

Catherine needed some air. She took photographs of the articles and clippings she'd discovered, then packed up her things and headed into the late afternoon. Unbeknownst to her, her feet led her directly to where her grandpa Gionnocaro and grandma Gwen had once lived and worked in the Upper East Side. The bakery had once been the meeting-point for locals, the place where coffee, bread, and sweets were shared and gossip was exchanged. But after her grandfather retired and long after her grandmother was gone, none of the children wanted to take over the bakery. They'd sold it to a dry cleaner. It was still running today.

In fact, standing there in front of the bakery, it was difficult to recall what it had once looked like. It was difficult to peel back the layers and consider that, once upon a time, two people had purchased this plot and opened a bakery.

If my grandfather wasn't really Gionnocaro, then who was he? Catherine thought now. Her eyes welled with tears. *And how does that change the identity of my entire family?*

Chapter Eleven

Scarlet and Nathan hopped off the ferry in Nantucket Harbor. Scarlet watched as Nathan struggled to draw his massive backpack onto his shoulders. Once he'd gotten it up, he straightened his spine and winked as though it were nothing to him.

"We should get a taxi," Scarlet said.

"You said you live right downtown!"

Scarlet winced. "Just looking at you makes my back hurt."

"I promise. I'm fine."

Scarlet led Nathan away from the docks, thick with sailboats and swarms of tourists with ice cream cones, through the teeming streets. Everything seemed in Technicolor. Tourists were over-tanned, and many of them bickered with each other about where to eat dinner or when to go back to the hotel.

"There's so much stress involved in vacation," Nathan muttered. "I remember that with my own family. It's nice they don't invite me anymore."

Scarlet grimaced and led him up a back staircase to

her little apartment. She flung the door open and led him inside. Once there, he shivered out of his backpack and rolled his shoulders back. "This is beautiful," he said of the place.

It wasn't much, but it was far nicer than the apartment Nathan had just abandoned in the Lower East Side. Big windows brought in soft yellow light, and white linen curtains flowed to the hardwood floor. A separate kitchen offered enough space for a little breakfast table, upon which Scarlet had put flowers that were now dried out but still pleasant. There were two bedrooms—a godsend, now that Nathan would be staying with her. Plus, there was a living room with a television and a big, soft couch.

When Nathan asked her what she paid for rent, his jaw dropped. "That's so cheap."

"It's not Manhattan," she reminded him.

Scarlet and Nathan splayed across the sofa for a few minutes with glasses of water. Nathan looked mesmerized, as though he still couldn't believe he'd left the city.

Scarlet contemplated their next steps. She itched to get out to the beach where the other Reddit poster had said the conservative hippie girls sometimes met. The plan was to take the video camera and capture as much of that scene as they could. Maybe they could approach a few of the hippie-dressed girls who arrived later and ask them a few pointed questions.

But what if they ran off? What if they refused to talk?

I don't know what I'm doing, Scarlet thought. *But fake it till you make it, right?*

Suddenly, a text came through on her phone. It was from her grandma Greta.

GRANDMA G: I heard a rumor you're
back in Nantucket. Why don't you come
over for dinner tonight?

"What's up?" Nathan asked, stretching his arms over his head.

"My grandma invited me over for dinner tonight."

Nathan arched his eyebrow. There was a beat of silence. "Isn't your grandma Greta Copperfield?"

Scarlet laughed. "Have you always known that?"

"I looked into it after Bernard Copperfield's book came out last year," Nathan confessed. "I couldn't believe it. I've known you for years and years, and I never knew you had these super-famous grandparents."

"Well, I didn't know them, either. But they're incredible." Scarlet took a breath. "Maybe we should go. Grandma's cooking is insane. It'll give us fuel for tonight."

Nathan's smile smeared off his face. "You want to film tonight already?"

"I want to try to find them, at least. No time like the present," Scarlet said. "And I'm sure you want to get a headstart on finding your sister."

Nathan bobbed his head. "To be honest, I'm having trouble getting it out of my head."

Scarlet squared her jaw. "Maybe we can film the interview with just you when the sun sets later tonight. It'll be good practice and get us in a better headspace for the project."

"Good idea."

Nathan and Scarlet showered quickly and changed into outfits better suited for an evening at The Copperfield House. Nathan had also read all about the artist residency and peppered Scarlet with questions on their walk over about how to apply.

"You have to have a project in mind," Scarlet explained. "My grandparents only approve artists or film-makers or writers or musicians who really speak to them. But for that reason, many of those same people are forever linked to The Copperfield House."

Scarlet briefly explained the story of Aurora from last year, how she'd come to the residency and had a brief breakdown that had resulted in the Copperfields taking her to a hospital.

"But now, she's basically like family," Scarlet explained. "She ended up with a guy here in Nantucket, and she comes over to talk to Grandma about art and music and writing a few times a week. Grandma is very generous with her time. I don't know how she does it. She juggles all the Copperfields and the new artists-in-residence, plus her own career."

"And you already said she cooks for everyone!" Nathan added.

"She's a better woman than me," Scarlet said.

Nathan flashed her a funny smile. "It sounds like you take after her to me."

Scarlet was delirious with joy to find her little brother on the beach outside The Copperfield House with a base-ball bat and a ball. Their cousin Danny was in the mid-distance with a baseball mitt, and Danny's sister Laura was a bit farther out, her dark hair flowing in the wind.

"We couldn't get enough people for a full game, so we're making it up as we go along," James explained as Scarlet and Nathan got closer.

Before Scarlet could say anything else, James tossed the ball into the air and smacked it with his bat. It went far, but not overly so; just far enough for Laura to run after it and catch it in her glove. Laura screamed with joy and jumped up and down.

But Scarlet knew that James had meant for her to catch it. "You have killer aim, bro."

James smiled that handsome Copperfield smile and turned his attention to Nathan.

"This is my brother, James," Scarlet explained. "James, this is Nathan, a friend from the city."

Nathan and James shook hands. Scarlet couldn't help but think her brother looked terribly adult.

"We didn't think you'd be back yet," James said to Scarlet.

"Mom stayed," Scarlet explained. "You know how she gets."

James's eyes widened. "Say no more."

Suddenly, Ivy whipped out the back porch. She wore a black swimsuit and thin sunglasses that barely covered her eyes. Her black hair was glossy and all the way to her waist.

"You're back?" Ivy hurried down the porch steps and side-hugged her sister and scrutinized Nathan.

"Mom stayed in the city," Scarlet explained. "This is Nathan."

"Ivy." Ivy slid her hand into Nathan's and frowned at him from behind her glasses. "Grandma's about to serve dinner. Help me set the table?"

Scarlet and Nathan followed Ivy back inside to fetch plates. From the hall, they heard Aunt Alana, Aunt Julia, and Aunt Ella bickering in the kitchen. Scarlet couldn't make out exactly what it was about, but she had a hunch Aunt Alana had caused the argument, and she was soon proven right.

"Just say I'm right and be done with it," Aunt Alana said, then burst into giggles.

Aunt Alana appeared with a big pot of buttery brussels sprouts and nearly ran into Ivy, Scarlet, and Nathan. "Oh! Scarlet's here, Mom!"

Alana whipped past, and Grandma Greta appeared a moment later to wrap Scarlet in a hug. Scarlet loved the way her grandmother smelled—always of whatever she'd recently been cooking, plus rosemary, thyme, and a hint of lavender.

"When your father said you were back, I knew I needed you here tonight," Grandma Greta said, squeezing Scarlet's shoulder. Her eyes then found Nathan. Her expression was difficult to read. "And who might this be?"

"This is Nathan, Grandma. He's a filmmaker," Scarlet said.

"Oh, good. We don't accept non-artists around here," Greta said, shaking Nathan's hand.

"That's the exact opposite of what my father said to me last Christmas," Nathan joked.

Greta looked taken aback. "How awful! What would he prefer you were doing?"

"Finance," Nathan said with an ironic laugh.

"Terrible. Just terrible." Greta clucked her tongue and carried on to the back porch, where the big table was set up for all the Copperfields who'd been able to come for dinner.

Scarlet, Ivy, and Nathan followed her and positioned the plates, forks, and spoons. Greta called the rest of the family up, and Aunt Julia and Aunt Ella brought out the fish, fresh bread, and sweet potatoes.

Scarlet watched Nathan fill his plate, then caught her

grandmother's eyes on him. Greta was smiling.

"I bought that from the Nantucket fish market this morning at five thirty," Greta told Nathan proudly.

"It looks divine," Nathan said. "Scarlet was saying you were a woman who wore many hats."

"It's just more interesting that way," Greta said, spooning herself a helping of sweet potatoes.

"Is Dad coming?" Scarlet asked Ivy, who sat beside her, looking glum.

Suddenly, Quentin's voice echoed out across the porch. "Was someone looking for me?" There he was in all his glory: the powerful Quentin Copperfield, wearing a suit, his black hair gelled, his eyes alert. He touched Ivy and Scarlet on the head, shook Nathan's hand briefly, and took a seat on the other side of Bernard.

"What a day," Quentin said, tearing a slice of bread. "We were up to our ears in interviews with this woman who lives outside of Woods Hole. We could not get her to tell the truth. It was so slippery. One minute, she would start a story we could back up with facts, and the next, she was out in left field, making something up."

Scarlet laughed. "How did you get her to tell the truth?"

"I don't know if we did," Quentin confessed. "But we got as close as we could."

"I was telling your wife about this recently," Greta said. "I don't believe in the truth. It's slippery. Maybe the woman you interviewed shares my belief."

"I don't think she thought about it that much," Quentin said. "She just wanted to make it into a better story."

"That's a great reason to lie, don't you think?" Grandma Greta said mischievously.

Nathan looked gleeful, as though he'd never heard an older woman promote lies before.

"How did it go at Ellis Island, Scarlet?" Greta asked then.

Scarlet swallowed a bite of lemony fish and considered how to explain what had happened. "Well, it didn't exactly go to plan."

Greta twisted to look at Quentin. "Did Catherine tell you that?"

"All Catherine told me was that she was hard at work," Quentin said, both hands up. "You know how she is when she's immersed in something. She doesn't want to talk about it. I get it. I'm the same way."

Greta turned to look at Scarlet again. "Go on."

"We thought we found him," Scarlet said. "It seemed easy. The only thing was, the Gionnocaro Fellini we found reached the United States in 1937 rather than 1942. But we figured maybe Mom's family got the date wrong."

Greta raised her eyebrows. It was clear she was captivated.

"But after that, Mom sent a picture of this 1937 Gionnocaro to her sister in Dubai. Aunt Sally said it was absolutely not him. It was the wrong Gionnocaro. So we went back to Ellis Island the next day to look for *our* Gionnocaro. But he wasn't there."

"Goodness," Greta said. "What a mystery."

"That's when Mom plunged into research without me," Scarlet said with a sad laugh. "Which was okay. I went to the movies and ran into an old friend." She nudged Nathan with the tip of her elbow. A shiver ran down her spine.

"What did you see?" her father asked.

"*Rear Window*," Scarlet said.

"A brilliant film. An absolute masterpiece," Quentin said.

"We agreed on that," Nathan affirmed.

Quentin smiled at Nathan in a way he never once had when Owen was around. Scarlet's heart swelled. She knew everyone at the table thought she and Nathan were in the throes of an August romance. The reality was far darker.

"Well, you know how your mother gets," Quentin said after a pause. "She gets obsessed. It's part of the reason I fell in love with her."

"You get obsessed, too," Scarlet reminded her father.

"Maybe it's the reason she fell in love with me, too," Quentin said.

"To me, all that work you guys do reminds me too much of writing research papers," Aunt Ella chimed in. "It reminds me of school."

Scarlet laughed and listened as the rest of her family's conversation consumed the table. Aunt Julia was "obsessed" with a new novel she was editing for the publishing house. Grandpa Bernard had just read an article about black holes that he would be thinking about for the rest of the day. Uncle Will had written three songs just that morning during a moment of either "inspiration or insanity." Nathan was able to chime in, then, and talk about the band he'd joined last year that had performed covers of Frank Zappa songs for "audiences that weren't ready for that yet."

Uncle Will burst into laughter that brought tears to his eyes. "Who is this kid?" he asked Scarlet, waving his fork. "He's hilarious."

After dinner, Scarlet helped clear the table, then

changed into her swimsuit and headed to the beach with Ivy, James, Nathan, Danny, and Laura. Immediately, Danny and Laura plunged into the water. Their laughter echoed.

Nathan pulled his shirt off to show a torso much more muscular than Scarlet had accounted for. When they'd first met again (just yesterday!), he'd said he'd gained weight from popcorn and snacks. It was unlikely.

"I'm going in!" he called, then ran off into the waves.

James joined, too. This left just Scarlet and Ivy on the sands in their swimsuits with the last of the orange August light on their shoulders. Ivy's expression was contemplative. Not for the first time this summer, Scarlet wondered what was on her sister's mind.

"How's it going?" Scarlet asked, trying to sound casual. "You ready to head back to NYU in a couple of weeks?"

Ivy sniffed and looked at the sand. She dug a hole with her thumb. "I don't know. To be honest, I really don't want to go back."

Scarlet hadn't expected this. Ivy had always been a go-getter in the truest sense, far more than Scarlet. When Scarlet had dropped out of college, she'd thought, *Ivy would never let this happen.*

"It's just a lot, you know?" Ivy said now of NYU. "It's an endless barrage of madness. I feel like I don't take a single breath from September to December."

This tugged at Scarlet's heartstrings. "Why haven't you said this before?"

Ivy shrugged and still refused to look at Scarlet.

Scarlet remembered something. "I mean, there's a different factor this year."

Ivy still didn't look up.

"You met someone," Scarlet said tenderly. "I know you're going to miss him."

Ivy let her shoulders droop. It was proof Scarlet was right.

Scarlet touched Ivy's shoulder. "Listen. I know it's rough to be in love and go

to school and try to do everything at once."

Ivy rolled her eyes.

"And I know you don't want my advice," Scarlet said with a soft laugh.

"I don't," Ivy said.

Scarlet removed her hand and started to dig her own hole in the sand. It was a distraction. "I'd love to meet this guy, you know."

"Yeah. Maybe soon," Ivy said.

"You want him all to yourself," Scarlet teased. "I remember what that was like. When I first met Owen, I was so possessive of him. I don't think we hung out with other friends for over a year. Stupidly, I thought one of my friends would try to steal him from me." She laughed nervously. "Obviously, I was very wrong about him. But I think you know what I mean."

"Maybe," Ivy said.

Scarlet exhaled all the air from her lungs. For a little while, she studied Ivy's profile—her soft cheeks and the sharp angle of her nose. How she loved this young woman! How she wanted to protect her!

We're getting further and further away from each other, Scarlet thought. *She knows how to protect herself.*

From the water, Nathan waved his hand and grinned madly. Scarlet felt the edges of her icy heart melt.

What a strange few days, she thought. She had no idea what would happen next.

Chapter Twelve

With her journalistic impulses ever more in tune, Catherine acted quickly. Before the afternoon was through, she had an address, and before evening fell, she was stationed in front of an Art Deco apartment building just five blocks from where she and Quentin had raised their three children. There she stood, heart pounding, checking the address twice more on her phone before proceeding to the doorman. The doorman looked respectable in his brown outfit and his low hat. He looked like the kind of man who always said hello to everyone and told them to have a wonderful day—and meant it.

It was the kind of building with apartments that cost upward of thirty million.

Catherine smiled at the doorman. She'd worn a suit jacket, a pencil skirt, and a pair of pearl earrings. She looked the part. "Hello. I'm here to see Rainer and April Fellini."

The doorman smiled and pressed the buzzer behind him, one that surely buzzed up in the Fellini apartment.

"Evening, madame," he said into a little golden phone. "I have a..." He cast Catherine a look that meant *who are you?*

"Catherine Copperfield."

"I have a Copperfield here to see you." The doorman furrowed his brow. "Very well. Thank you." He then returned the phone to its cradle and turned to open the door for Catherine. "The Fellinis are in the penthouse apartment. All the way up."

Catherine found herself in a lobby from another time. A golden clock kept perfect time; royal red velvet sofas lined the walls; beautiful and ornate plants burst in bright greens as though they got more sun down here than they possibly could have. Catherine reached the elevator and pressed the button for the top floor. But when the elevator arrived, there was a traditional elevator operator inside. She wondered if it was for added security—or just to give the old apartment building a touch of old-world whimsy.

The rich really do live differently, she thought, then remembered that she and Quentin were also wealthy. Because she hadn't grown up that way, it was sometimes difficult to remember that she was now firmly in that camp.

The elevator opened directly into Rainer and April Fellini's penthouse apartment. The apartment had originally belonged to Stephan, Rainer's father, until Stephan suffered a major stroke last year and required Rainer and April to move in. Rainer and April had three children, the eldest of whom was a twenty-one-year-old woman named Felicity. Catherine had gleaned this information during three hours of online sleuthing.

Catherine was accustomed to investigating like this. It was the nature of her journalistic work.

But it was bizarre to sleuth with her family's story in mind.

April Fellini met Catherine in the lobby. She wore a soft linen outfit, and her face would have been beautiful if it weren't so pinched and sorrowful. She was maybe in her fifties, slightly older than Catherine. She tried to smile.

"Good evening," she said. "Welcome to our home."

"Thank you." Catherine clutched the strap of her tote bag.

Over the phone, she'd said she wanted to interview the Fellini family about Gionnocaro Fellini's remarkable work in the field of academia prior to his early death. She'd lied to say her book project was about the incredibly dense history of NYU academia and how immigrants from countries all over the world had contributed to it.

They'd taken the bait easily. Everyone wanted to believe their family members were more important to history than they actually were.

"You're a novelist," April said, raising her chin. "I always wanted to write a novel."

"I'm a journalist, actually," Catherine said. "This is my first book."

"How exciting." April sounded distracted. "Rainer is in the living room. Stephan should wake up from his nap in about twenty minutes. We can bring him out then." She hesitated and wrung her hands. "I'm sorry to say that it's essential we uphold Stephan's schedule. He's getting better, but it's a slow process."

"I understand," Catherine assured her.

Rainer stood when they entered the living room. Although she'd seen photos of him online, Catherine was startled by how much he looked like his grandpa Gionno-caro. Catherine shook his hand. His eyes looked lost.

It feels like I'm somewhere I shouldn't be, Catherine thought.

"Good evening," Rainer said as Catherine sat down. "Did you come to the city just for this project?"

Catherine saw no reason to lie more than she already had. "I lived here for many years," Catherine said. "I raised my children not far from here. Recently, my husband and I relocated to Nantucket Island, and I don't get back as often as I'd like. This project was a great excuse."

"How nice," Rainer said. He cleared his throat. "Tell me. What clued you in on my grandfather? Despite his tremendous background and intellect, he's rarely mentioned at all in academic papers or academic histor-ical journals. He died before he could make any real impact, I'm afraid."

"It's a real tragedy," Catherine said. She searched her mind for how to explain without giving her game away. "To be honest, my own grandfather was also an immi-grant from Italy. He had tremendous skills in his home-land, none of which translated to what he could do professionally here. He floundered for years and then opened a bakery that just barely kept him and his family afloat. That fact forced me to reckon with a clear problem of immigrants here in New York City."

"Underappreciated," Rainer said with a sniff. It was clear from his expression that he'd bought what Catherine sold him.

Catherine spent ten minutes asking Rainer and April questions about Gionnocaro's research; about his time at

NYU; about the awards he'd won at the university before his untimely death eight years after his arrival.

Very soon, it was time for the main event. April went down the hallway to collect Stephan. "I know he'll want to talk to you about his father," April said. There was a soft glint in her eyes.

Still, something is off about this family. I can't put my finger on it, Catherine thought.

Rainer and Catherine made small talk while April got Stephan around. It turned out they'd once belonged to the same gym down the road; they both liked the same Mexican restaurant in the neighborhood. Catherine tried to keep a wide berth from mention of her husband. The minute Quentin Copperfield came into the conversation, people were bound to have a different opinion about her.

I just want to be Catherine, the journalist.

April brought Stephan down the hall in his wheelchair a few minutes later. Despite his stroke last year, he was bright-eyed and smiling. April had said his brain worked like a machine these days. The physical therapy had helped a great deal, as had the memory exercises he did with his son and grandson every morning over breakfast. These intimate details almost overwhelmed Catherine. *This is a family. It's not my family, but there's tremendous love here. How dare I break in and lie to them?*

But she had to know the truth.

Stephan took Catherine's hand and beamed at her. "I hear you're trying to get my father's name out there again. I can't thank you enough."

Catherine's cheeks hurt from fake smiling. "He deserves it."

April set Stephan's chair up beside Rainer's and went

to the kitchen to fetch glasses of mint lemonade with fresh ice. This left Catherine with the son and grandson of the original Gionnocaro Fellini. A lump formed in her throat.

She forced herself to ask Stephan a few easy questions about his childhood before launching into what she wanted to know. Stephan jumped through them like hoops, and then carried on, saying, "You know, when my father was back in Italy, he was born to a princess and prince and enjoyed a truly stupendous life. Everything he wanted, he could have. Divine food. Full-fat milk during times of war. Dessert after dessert. And of course, all the women were after him because he had this royal title."

Stephan went on to tell several stories that Catherine had already heard—the one about Gionnocaro Fellini losing his horse in the middle of Tuscany and hitchhiking back to his castle; the one about Gionnocaro Fellini accidentally losing his mother's ring during a round of poker and having to fight the guy to get the ring back; the one about Gionnocaro Fellini proposing to the princess of Norway, only for her to rebuke him and marry the prince of Sweden at that time.

Of course, Catherine's grandfather had told her these stories, too. But he'd always told them as though they were his own.

They were identical.

But Catherine could see how thrilled Stephan was to share these stories with her. It was remarkable. Catherine could have finished any of the stories herself because she knew them by heart. But if she had, she would have given herself away.

Stephan, Rainer, and April sat in steady silence after Stephan's last story. Stephan looked very pleased with himself.

Catherine remembered to say, "These stories are truly incredible. I know they'll find their way into the book. Thank you so much for sharing them."

"My father would love that his stories live on like this," Stephan said. Tears twinkled in his eyes. "He was an extraordinary man. It breaks my heart that I never got to really know him."

Catherine smiled and cleared her throat. It was time to ask what she'd come here to find out. But she wanted to be delicate.

"Through my research, I learned that there was a question of foul play in Gionnocaro's death. It sounds like your mother, Dee Fellini, didn't want any postmortem tests performed. Can you speak to that?"

Stephan's cheeks went slack. Rainer twitched and scratched behind his ear. Silence fell over them.

But Catherine had come to ask this. She wouldn't leave before she knew.

Finally, as women always do, April swooped in to save the day. "The family is quite split about that story," she said.

Catherine raised her eyebrows. "I see."

"It's difficult," Rainer agreed. "Nobody wants to believe anything sour went on. The fact that my grandmother wanted him to be buried immediately speaks to her religious upbringing more than anything else. She didn't want to hide anything from the police. She was just brokenhearted."

Stephan hung his head and studied his knees. Catherine's hands were in fists.

"Do you happen to remember an early nanny you had, Stephan?" she asked. "Her name was Gwen."

Stephan met her gaze. "Maybe. Maybe a little bit."

He frowned. "I seem to remember her teaching me how to ride a bicycle. And maybe there was roller-skating in the park?"

Catherine's heart swelled. Still, it felt unfair that this stranger had memories of her grandmother that she was never allowed to have.

Did Gwen kill Gionnocaro? Catherine shivered.

"Why do you ask?" Stephan asked.

"I'm just trying to get a clear picture of who might have been in the apartment at the time of his death," Catherine said.

"My mother, my sister, and I were in the Hamptons. I assume that means our nanny was with us, too," Stephan pointed out.

Catherine nodded. "But the newspaper article I read said that a staff member disappeared after your father's death."

Stephan's eyes looked far away. It was clear Catherine had stirred up turmoil.

"You know," April stuttered, "I really think that's enough, don't you?" She looked at Rainer hopefully. She clearly wanted him to take over.

Rainer sat glumly with his large hands on his thighs.

"You should talk to my mother," Stephan said.

Catherine's eyebrows shot toward her hairline. *Dee? Dee's still alive?* It seemed insane.

"She lives in a nursing home in the Upper East Side," Stephan said. "Her brain is better than mine is. She'll outlive us all."

Catherine hadn't even thought to check on Dee. She'd assumed she was gone.

"Will this sort of conversation bother her too much?" Catherine asked, nervous that Dee was too old to handle it. She didn't want to barge into a nursing home and demand too much of a little old lady.

Stephan barked with laughter. Even Rainer smiled.

"Grandma is something else," Rainer admitted. "She can handle just about everything."

Catherine remembered the photographs of Gionnocaro's young wife with a grim smile. Like Gionnocaro, Dee had been in academia, as well.

"Maybe she'll find her way into your book," Stephan said after a pause. "She was just as brilliant as Father was. But people didn't pay as much attention. She was a woman in a man's world, you see."

"Like me," Catherine said, closing her notebook. She suddenly needed to get out of there. She needed to breathe fresh air and walk the streets.

Catherine asked to use the bathroom before she left. She didn't want to go immediately back to her hotel. Besides, she hoped to see a few more photos of Gionnocaro in the hallway.

April said, "It's the second door to the left down that hall."

Catherine got up and went to the bathroom. But there were no photographs in the hall save for one of a regal-looking hunting dog.

Catherine washed her hands and re-emerged to overhear April's tear-filled voice. "I just don't understand it."

Catherine stopped short in the shadows of the hallway. *Did I cause this?* Shame came over her. *I shouldn't have barged in here like this. I shouldn't have meddled.*

"There's no note in her bedroom?" Stephan asked.

Catherine was worried she'd be caught spying, so she proceeded down the hall and smiled nervously at April. April's face was streaked with tears.

"Goodness, I'm embarrassed," April said, hopping up from her chair and guiding Catherine to the elevator.

Catherine was at a loss for words. It was clear, now, that April's tears had nothing to do with her. Whatever this was about was probably why the family had seemed so glum earlier. Talk of Gionnocaro had distracted them for a time. But it hadn't lasted.

Catherine braved a last question. "Are you all right, April?"

They stood next to the elevator, waiting for it to come up from floor five.

April pressed her eyes into her sleeve. Her shoulders shuddered. "You said you have children."

"I do. Three."

April sniffed. "Our eldest girl, Felicity, ran out on us. She refuses to go back to college."

Catherine felt frozen with sorrow. She remembered Scarlet, who'd dropped out of NYU when Catherine's chemo had taken over her life. But this sounded different.

"When did this happen?" Catherine asked.

"She left school before the semester ended in April. We thought it was a breakdown of some kind. We sent money. We begged her to come home. She's strung us along all summer long. But she still won't tell us where she is. We even hired a private investigator, but it's like she's off the grid. We have no idea what's happened," April said. "Every once in a while, she contacts us again for money, and we send it because we're so worried. But how long can this go on? If she's really in need of money, she's using us. Maybe she'll never come back." April let out a horrible wail.

Catherine couldn't help but gather April in her arms. April shook and cried until the elevator appeared. Then she pulled away, fixed her face, and stared at the ground. "Thank you for coming by. Good luck with Dee. She expects you. You'll let us know when the book is finished, won't you?"

"I'll let you know," Catherine promised. She stepped on the elevator, and then she was gone.

Chapter Thirteen

Scarlet and Nathan left The Copperfield House that evening at eight forty-five. They were the last of those who didn't live there to depart for the night. That hadn't been their plan. But Greta had asked perhaps fifty questions of Nathan about his ideas surrounding film and his future hopes and dreams. This was the way of Greta Copperfield. To Scarlet's surprise, Nathan didn't squirm or flinch away from the questions. He was happy to talk.

To Grandma Greta, he'd said, "I have ten or fifteen different ideas for films, but the problem is, living in the city means I never have enough cash to make even a short film to enter into a contest. It's difficult. I don't know how anyone breaks through. And like I was telling Scarlet before, I really hate Los Angeles. I don't see myself there."

Greta's eyes had glinted in that way of hers; proof she was already invested in this young man's future. She'd said, "That's where The Copperfield House comes in. Let's talk soon about getting you in for a residency!"

Now, as Nathan and Scarlet strolled through the cool night air, Nathan said, "It feels fortuitous that I met your grandma and grandpa. They make me believe in something. A better future for myself." He paused and gave Scarlet a sheepish smile.

"They have that effect on almost everyone," Scarlet admitted. "I'm sure it was tricky being their children. They just want so much for everyone. They don't accept anything but the very best effort."

Nathan nodded. As they walked, his hand brushed against Scarlet's. "I can't believe I wasted so much time in New York City, working those dead-end jobs."

"You're only twenty-four," Scarlet reminded him. "Grandma always says we have more time than we think. We just have to use it."

"Only twenty-four, with my whole life ahead of me," Nathan said. "Just yesterday, I thought I was doomed. That's when you walked through the doors of the cinema."

They returned to Scarlet's place to grab their film equipment and Scarlet's car, then drove out to the beach directly beside Miacomet Beach, where the Reddit user suggested that the conservative hippie-dressed girls meet after sunset. They didn't have much time. Scarlet set up a foldable beach chair, attached a microphone to Nathan's breast pocket, and set him up so that a purple sunset spread out behind his shoulders and erupted to a black sky filled with stars directly above him. It was the perfect time to film the interview.

Nathan turned into a performer immediately. Although he took the material very seriously—it was his sister, Maddie, after all—he spoke animatedly in a way that would ultimately bring the documentary material alive.

After he'd described what happened that night in his parents' apartment, Scarlet decided to go off script a little bit. For the sake of the documentary and for the sake of her own curiosity.

"What do you think they're really up to?" she asked.

Nathan clenched his jaw and turned his head so his nose was in line with the water behind him. "I've thought about this a lot," he said, his tone deep. "What we know now is that young women between the ages of, say, eighteen and twenty-three disappear seemingly on purpose, yet continue to ask for money from their very wealthy parents. We also speculate that those wealthy parents are too embarrassed about the situation to alert the police. That, and the young women in question—including my sister—are in contact enough with the parents to ensure that nobody panics too, too much."

"Right," Scarlet said from the other side of the shot.

"My best guess is that it's some kind of political protest," Nathan said. "These young women are so privileged that they can't see beyond themselves. But they want to believe they stand for something. So they get rid of their material possessions. They leave their university. But it turns out that they still need money, so they continue to ask for it. Maybe they're pooling all of it to live together, where they have meetings on political justice and feminism and things like that. But they can't see that they're still in a bubble. It's just that they've formed a new bubble without the guidance of their parents. They think they're revolutionists, but they're just runaways."

Scarlet was breathless. She cut the shot and gaped at Nathan. What he'd just said rang so many bells for her.

"I can't pretend that I thought much differently than that when I was younger," she said after a long silence.

Nathan raised his shoulders. "We all thought like that."

"Not all of us joined 'cults' or whatever this is," Scarlet said.

Nathan bowed his head. His expression was thoughtful.

Scarlet thought, *He's the real deal. He refused money from his parents. He actually stepped out on his own.*

And then she remembered—again—that she'd refused her parents' money when she got her own apartment. Her heart lifted. *Maybe I'm a better person than I thought.*

Slowly, Scarlet and Nathan drove from this beach to the one directly beside it. Miacomet Beach. She cut the engine and rolled down the windows. It was time to wait.

A stakeout.

Night fell quickly. One minute, Scarlet could make out the sweep of the water along the sands, and the next, it was pitch black. She and Nathan sat in a comfortable silence, waiting. She wondered how long they would wait. An hour? Three hours? There was no telling if the conservative hippie-dressed young women remained in Nantucket at all. Perhaps they'd boarded a boat and gone elsewhere. Perhaps it was a smaller group than they suspected.

Maybe they'd already gotten into some kind of argument and disbanded.

There goes my only idea for a documentary, Scarlet thought selfishly. *Now what?*

Nathan quit his jobs for this?

But suddenly, Scarlet heard something and twisted to spot dark figures coming down the beach. "Get the camera," she breathed.

Nathan hurried to set up the camera from the passenger side. He started rolling.

There were maybe fifty or sixty of them. A man toward the front carried a torch, and a few others carried flashlights. It was difficult to make out the others until they set up the bonfire and lit it. As the fire crawled over the tinder, it flashed light across what had to be thirty or forty young women with very long hair, dressed in old-fashioned hippie-esque clothing. The women flowed through the crowd, talking to one another gently. Smiling. Sometimes they danced to music Scarlet couldn't quite hear.

The men were another story. There were twenty or thirty of them dressed in black. They were anywhere from eighteen to thirty years old. From here, it looked to Scarlet as though the men were in charge.

Did they tell the wealthy young women how to "start a political protest"?

Were they manipulating the young women and stealing their parents' money?

Scarlet's heartbeat intensified. She was reminded of Woodstock, of joyful celebrations in the sixties and seventies. But something about this was sinister.

These young women had been given the world. They'd been born into endless wealth and prosperity. They were rejecting it. But they weren't rejecting it the way Nathan had. What were they doing it for? For a little party on the beach?

Suddenly, one of the men got up on a large rock and

spread his hands out. The crowd quieted and formed a circle around him to hear him speak.

"We have to get over there," Scarlet breathed. "We have to hear what he's saying."

Nathan muttered under his breath.

"What?" Scarlet asked. "Nathan?"

Nathan turned his head too quickly and winced. "I wish I could see my sister. But they all look the same."

Scarlet touched his shoulder gently. Her heart ached for him. *Ivy's friend from school is over there. Maybe she's having the time of her life. Perhaps she's being held against her will. How do I figure that out?*

How do I make a documentary that explores the nature of this "organization"?

Everything felt terribly difficult all of a sudden. Scarlet's hands were in fists.

A smack rang out. Scarlet turned to find a large hand on the front window of her car. Behind that hand was the leering face of a man dressed all in black. He looked at her as though he knew all about her. The sound of him hitting her car continued to echo through her ears.

"What the heck?" Nathan cried out. His camera was pointed directly at the man.

"What the heck, indeed," the man said. Scarlet guessed he was twenty-five or twenty-six. His eyes were dark green and lined with red. "What are you doing here?"

"We're just hanging out at the beach," Scarlet said. She hated how much her voice shook.

"Oh? Well, this is a private beach tonight," the man said sweetly. "Do you mind moving on down the road?"

"This is a public beach," Scarlet retorted. "We have every right to be here."

"What are you doing over there?" Nathan demanded. "What is that man saying?"

The man at their car gave them a slippery smile. Scarlet's heart skipped a beat. *He's a sociopath,* she thought.

"If I were you, which I'm not," the man said sweetly, "I'd move along as quickly as I could."

"Or what?" Nathan demanded.

"I wouldn't want to wait around to find out," the man said. "But that's just me! We're all different."

"It doesn't look like everyone's different in your cult," Nathan shot.

The man's eyes flickered strangely. Scarlet realized she'd never been so frightened of anyone in her life. Not even Owen.

"Let's go, Nathan," Scarlet whispered. She hoped it wasn't loud enough for the man to hear.

But he did hear.

"You'd better listen to your little lady here," the man said. "It sounds like she's the logical one in this relationship. What a pity."

Scarlet's ears rang. *They're sexist. That's clear.*

Scarlet turned the key in the ignition and revved the engine. The man stepped back with his hands raised. He still wore that sinister smile. Scarlet thought she'd see it again and again in her nightmares. As tears filled her eyes, she slammed her foot on the gas and took them away from the beach. All the while, Nathan filmed, even leaning outside the window to get the last of that horrible man as he watched them drive away.

Chapter Fourteen

Scarlet and Nathan didn't speak the entire drive back to the apartment. Nathan clutched the video camera with starkly white fingers, and Scarlet had to focus extra hard on the road lest she run a red light or miss a stop sign. She knew Nantucket like the back of her hand these days. But she was also frantic and out of her mind. She had to make it home. *Breathe, Scarlet,* she told herself.

Back in the living room, Scarlet opened all the windows to take in the cool night air and played a vinyl in the record player to calm her mind. Nathan took a shower and then stretched himself out on the floor. It was clear they were both too frightened to make sense of what had just happened.

It was eleven forty-five before Nathan sat up and said, "I think we should go back."

Scarlet gaped at him. She wanted to ask, *are you out of your mind?*

"It would allow us the element of surprise. I don't think they'd expect us," he said. "Maybe we could even creep closer and see if my sister is there. Maybe we can hear what they're saying."

Scarlet's heart pounded too quickly. She sat on the floor and touched Nathan's hand. She saw worry for his sister swimming through his eyes.

"I didn't know how big this was," Scarlet said tentatively. "I'm beginning to think we should go to the police."

Nathan bowed his head.

"That guy scared me," Scarlet breathed. "It was like he saw all the way through me. It made me think that he recruited these young women. He has that kind of personality."

"Sociopathic," Nathan said, repeating what she'd already thought.

"Yes." Scarlet closed her eyes and placed her head next to Nathan's on the rug.

They lay and stared at the crack in the ceiling. Scarlet thought, *Maybe I don't have what it takes to make a documentary after all. Perhaps I don't have my mother's keen intuition.*

Nathan touched her hair. The act was so tender that Scarlet burrowed closer to him and wrapped her arm around his chest. She listened to the thud of his heart.

"I don't know about going to the police yet," Nathan said after a time. "As far as we know, they haven't actually done anything against the law yet. And if they think the police are after them, they'll go somewhere else. They'll escape to another island or another city. We'll lose them."

Scarlet understood. She closed her eyes as tightly as she could as her ears rang.

Nathan's voice was very quiet. "We have good footage from today, though. If you still want to try to make this documentary."

Scarlet propped her head up with her elbow and studied Nathan's face. It was hard to fathom that this was the same fourteen-year-old boy she'd first kissed.

"It's hard to make a documentary when I don't know what's at stake," she breathed. "I don't know how dangerous it is. For us or for the girls."

Nathan nodded. "Let's get a little bit closer. Let's keep filming. Let's push it. Perhaps we'll catch them doing something. Maybe we can call the police immediately and have them all arrested like that." He snapped his fingers.

"The element of surprise," Scarlet repeated.

"Exactly."

Scarlet was exhausted. She limped through her nightly ritual of washing her face and brushing her teeth. She'd already put fresh sheets on Nathan's bed. She stood in the doorway of his bedroom and peered inside, where he sat up against the pillows and read a few pages in a book. It felt bizarre. They were playing house, but they also weren't.

For whatever reason, she really wanted him to come to her bedroom. But she also knew that was impossible.

"Good night," Scarlet said.

"Sleep well, Scarlet." Nathan closed his book on his thumb and raised his chin to look at her.

Scarlet's heart thumped.

"Thank you for bringing me here," Nathan said. "Now that I've seen what kind of people they are, it's like I have a fire under me. I have to bring my sister home."

Scarlet set her jaw. She knew he wasn't doing it for his parents' sake, nor for his parents' love. He was doing it because it was the right thing.

It was rare to meet people like Nathan in this world.

"I have a terrible feeling we're in over our heads," Scarlet whispered.

"We have each other," Nathan reminded her. "It'll be all right."

Scarlet prayed that was true.

Chapter Fifteen

Catherine woke up the following morning at her traditional time and ran longer than usual around Central Park and its surrounding neighborhoods. A part of her hoped to run into Rainer or April by accident, if only to pester them with more questions about Dee and Gionnocaro and the potential that Gionnocaro's death wasn't fate. But all she saw were the typical park runners and mothers and babysitters; the birdwatchers and the baseball players trying to cram a game in before work.

Catherine called Quentin when she got back to the hotel that morning. They'd spoken on the phone every other day or so since she'd arrived. Quentin knew how immersed she was. He got the same way about his projects. There were no hard feelings.

Quentin's voice was warm and loving. She wanted to cuddle up against him and tell him everything.

"How are you, my love?" Quentin asked.

"It's all much harder than anticipated," Catherine

said, laughing at herself. It was a laugh she didn't truly feel.

"Isn't it always?"

Catherine splayed across her hotel bed. It was a different room than the initial one she'd rented, as she'd downsized after Scarlet left spontaneously.

"Have you seen our girl?" Catherine asked.

"I did. She had a boy with her."

Catherine smiled into the phone. "I wondered if something like that had happened. What was he like?"

"He was very kind. Patient with my mother's endless questions. Good dresser. Funny. Ate all the food on his plate and even ate a second portion when my mother pushed it on him."

Catherine giggled. "Sounds like he's Greta-approved."

"Rumor has it she wants him at The Copperfield House soon," Quentin said.

"Wow. So she *really* likes him."

"Seems like it."

Catherine smiled. All she'd wanted was for Scarlet to get over Owen. All she'd wanted was for her daughter to see the light at the end of the horrific tunnel that was being in your mid-twenties.

"I have another interview this afternoon," Catherine said.

"Who's it with?" Quentin asked.

"Complicated question. Complicated answer."

Quentin laughed. "You know you can run through this with me whenever you want."

"I'll let you know."

Catherine decided to take it easy that morning. She grabbed breakfast at a diner down the road and read the

New York Times cover to cover, then walked through a few shopping districts and imagined a future in which her book was a bestseller, and she truly understood who it was her grandfather and grandmother had been.

Were they really con artists who'd killed the original Gionnocaro Fellini? She'd deal with that when she came to it.

Of course, that reality would sell books. But it would also break her mother's heart.

It was already starting to break hers. It tainted her memories of her beloved grandfather. Hearing her own grandfather's stories from Rainer and Stephan had been exhilarating and terrifying and heartbreaking.

Whose stories belong to whom?

Catherine entered the chill of the Upper East Side Elder Care Home at five minutes to three that afternoon. She knew Dee Fellini expected her. April had arranged it.

The fact that Dee was still so whip-smart and spry spoke to a theme within this story. All the women involved were quite intellectual, including her own mother. Including herself. *Women are truly something else.*

The only one missing is Gwen.

A nurse in red scrubs walked Catherine to the back hall of the home to a large apartment with FELLINI written on the door. The nurse knocked and said, "Dee? You have a visitor!" in an overly bright and false voice. Catherine wondered what it was like to get old like that; to have such knowledge about the world and get treated like a child.

Dee was dressed immaculately in a powder-blue sweater and a pair of linen slacks. Her makeup was precise and powerful, and she wore a color of lipstick that evoked sophistication. The way she looked at Catherine now reminded Catherine of regal cats.

It wasn't so hard to peer beyond this old woman's face and find the young woman beneath—the young woman from the photos of the wedding and the baby showers. The young academic who'd had it all before her husband had died.

His death must have broken her heart, Catherine thought. *She never remarried.*

"Good afternoon," Catherine said. She wanted to sound demure.

"Hello." Dee remained seated.

"You'll let me know if you need anything, won't you, Dee?" the nurse asked.

"Yes. As always." Dee waved her hand.

The nurse left Catherine alone with Dee. Catherine had never been so nervous in her life—and she'd interviewed numerous celebrities and politicians.

"Have a seat," Dee ordered.

"Thank you." Catherine sat across from her and pulled out her notebook.

"My daughter-in-law tells me you're writing a book about academics at NYU," Dee said.

"That's right."

"Tell me. What led you to Gionnocaro?" Dee asked.

The way she said his name was beautiful. She pronounced it in perfect Italian.

Catherine repeated what she'd told Rainer and April. "Of course, I'm well aware that you're an academic in your own right. I'm pleased to include both you and your husband in the book. Maybe you were one of the first intellectual married couples in the city."

Dee slid her tongue over her false teeth. "Nobody ever recorded what a miserable academic Gionnocaro was, I suppose."

Catherine was taken aback yet terribly pleased. She hadn't expected this. Vitriol was the only word for it.

Dee laughed wickedly. "Gionnocaro had no idea what he was doing when he arrived in America. He'd been a royal back in Italy. He'd eaten pastries and dated princesses and traveled all over. But he knew nothing about research. He knew nothing about academia."

Catherine remembered his photo at Ellis Island. "Didn't he list himself as an academic at Ellis Island?"

Dee's eyes flickered with curiosity. "You've seen his portrait at Ellis Island?"

"I looked into all of the immigrants I want to feature in my book," she lied.

"Yes, well. Like I said. Gionnocaro's wealth allowed him to say whatever he wanted to be. When he started at NYU, he floundered around like a fool. He would have been a laughing stock if he hadn't met me." Dee smiled in a way that meant she was terribly pleased with herself.

"That's fascinating. He got away with it, then?" Catherine said. "Like you said, I never saw any mention of him as a *bad academic*."

"A handsome man like that could get away with anything," Dee said. "And the stories he told! He could captivate a room."

"Your son and grandson might have mentioned a few of the stories," Catherine said. Her throat felt tight.

"It's been so many years since he died, and his stories live on," Dee said. "He was never meant to be an academic. Maybe he was never meant to be a husband or a father. But he was meant to tell stories." Dee smiled to herself. "You know, a part of me wanted to go to Italy and actually look into those stories. Were they real? Probably half of them weren't, but he had the wealth to back up the royalty claim, which was wonderful. I'd never really had much to my name. Suddenly, I was awash with wealth. Suddenly, I had a house in the Hamptons. Suddenly, I was *one of those women*. It terrified me."

Catherine could relate, although she decided not to say so.

How was she going to broach the topic of Gwen?

That was when it occurred to her.

If Dee had grown up without money, was it possible she'd known Gwen during that pre-Gionnocaro time?

Was that how Gwen had come into her life in the first place?

But Catherine didn't have time to ask. Suddenly, a nurse entered the room and said, "Dee? It's time for poker."

Dee waved her hand. "Those people don't know how to play poker."

It was clear she meant the other people in elder care.

"I know. But they rely on you to remind them of the rules," the nurse said with a funny smile.

"Don't coddle me," Dee scolded.

Catherine had to fight not to smile. But it seemed this had convinced Dee, for now. She rose grandly, then took a walker and led Catherine down the hall to the poker tournament. "We have it once a week," she explained. "It's true that most of them forget the rules week to week. Alzheimer's, dementia, they have just about everything under the sun. I'll never know why I was spared. Genetics, I suppose. My mother and grandmother both lived till they were one hundred and one and were present every day of their lives."

"That's incredible."

"What about your family?" Dee asked.

Catherine was surprised by the question. She was the one looking into Dee's family, not the other way around.

"My mother is as smart as they come," Catherine said. "She's an academic, too."

"And you're a journalist."

"Yes." Catherine smiled.

"And your husband?" Dee asked.

Catherine felt embarrassed. She didn't want to say who he was. "He's a

journalist, too. That's how we met." It wasn't a lie.

"Good. It's good to marry someone who matches your intellect," Dee said.

In marrying Gionnocaro, Dee had not.

They reached the community room, where nurses dressed in faux-bartender outfits had set up poker games. Dee went to the first table and sat down, gesturing for the seat beside her. It was meant for Catherine. Catherine felt floaty and strange. She was probably at least forty years younger than everyone else in the room besides the nurses. A woman with a walker came toward their table, stopped, and looked at Dee. She clicked her jaw.

"Are you going to sit down, Winnie?" Dee asked. She sounded exasperated.

Winnie took the seat on the opposite side of Dee. She remained quiet.

"Do you remember the rules this week, Winnie?" Dee asked. Her tone was softer than it had been.

Winnie took a breath. "It's coming back to me. Slowly but surely."

Dee shifted to look at Catherine. "Winnie was diagnosed with something nasty earlier this year. We're doing our best to fight it. Keep the brain active." She clicked the tip of her finger against her forehead. "But time only marches forward."

Winnie stared at the cards as they flicked out across the table.

"We used to run this joint," Dee said. "Winnie and me. We had an epic rivalry. Lots of trash talk across the table." Dee winked.

Catherine sensed that, for all of Dee's hardness, she truly loved the woman beside her. Perhaps they'd lived here at the Elder Care Home for a number of years, gossiping and remembering and squeezing the last gorgeous moments of their lives out of what they had left.

The poker game began. Catherine wanted to prove herself to Dee; to prove she at least had a mind for cards. She was pleased when she won the first round. Dee's eyes shimmered.

"Not bad," Dee said. "You've played before."

Catherine didn't answer. Dee seemed to like that, too.

The game went on. Catherine got swept up in it, noting that she, Dee, and a guy in his late eighties at their table were the only ones really in it. Dee shot trash talk to the guy, who whipped it right back. It was almost as though they were flirting. Catherine hoped so. Dee had lost her husband seventy years ago, for crying out loud. She deserved a little male attention.

Thirty minutes into the game, the nurses announced a break with cookies and punch. Dee reached over to touch Winnie's shoulder and say something soft and kind that Catherine couldn't hear. Catherine took a cookie with white chocolate chips and nibbled at the edges. It was just as good as the cookies from a typical Upper East Side bakery; far better than anything taken from a plastic container. *Upper-echelon of elder care.*

When Dee turned her head back to Catherine, Catherine decided not to hesitate. It was time.

"By the way," Catherine said, "do you remember a young woman who worked for you back in the early forties? Gwen?"

Dee stitched her eyebrows together. A beat passed. "Say that name again?"

"Gwen." Catherine set down the rest of her cookie. Just as with Greta, she struggled to comprehend what was really going on behind Dee's eyes. "She worked as a nanny for you after Stephan was born, I think."

"Gosh, we had so many people working for us back then," Dee said with a wave of her hand. "Like I said, wealth was a totally new concept for me. People milled in and out of our apartment. They knew more of what we owned than I did. What with my studies and the children, I barely kept myself above water."

Catherine realized that Dee no longer looked her in the eye. Catherine's throat tightened. *Dee's lying,* she thought, but she wasn't sure why she knew that so clearly.

Suddenly, Winnie piped up. "Gwen? Isn't that the woman who tried to rob you?"

Dee twisted around to glare at Winnie. It was the first time Winnie had said anything coherent enough for Catherine to hear.

Dee looked mystified, then enraged. "No. Nobody tried to rob us, darling." But there was a hard edge to her voice.

Catherine's heartbeat quickened. She remembered the newspaper article stating that staff members had disappeared after Gionnocaro's death.

What wasn't Dee telling Catherine? What had Dee been hiding when she'd wanted Gionnocaro buried immediately?

Catherine had been doing this too long not to know there was a deep and powerful story behind these lies.

Suddenly, Dee's mouth opened into a yawn. She closed her eyes and stretched her arms over her head.

What a great actress, Catherine thought.

"Catherine, it's been wonderful chatting with you," Dee said. "But I really must be getting back to my room. All this card-playing takes it right out of me."

Catherine tried not to give herself away. She crossed her arms over her chest and smiled. "I appreciate the time we spent together. I hope we can talk more about the book soon."

Dee's eyes flickered as though she no longer believed Catherine was writing a book about *academia.*

The question about Gwen gave the game away.

Catherine excused herself directly from the community room and headed for the lobby. She knew in her bones this wouldn't be her final trip to visit Dee. But she wasn't sure where to go from here.

Suddenly, Catherine's phone lit up with a call from April Fellini, of all people. Was she checking up on Catherine? Or had Dee already contacted April to tell her *don't let that woman near me again?*

April's voice warbled and was filled with tears. "Catherine?"

Catherine stopped at the exit with her hand on the metal door. "April. Is everything all right?"

April sniffled. "It's just that... you're a journalist, right?"

"Yes."

"And you have children. You said you have children. You raised them in our neighborhood?" April said.

Catherine furrowed her brow and stepped into the sunlight outside the Elder Care Home. "That's right. Just a few blocks away."

April stuttered. "It's just that we don't want to alert the cops. We know Felicity left of her own volition. And we know we sent her money because we *want* to. We want to know she's safe. But we really need her to come home, Catherine. We can't handle it anymore. My health is failing. My husband can't sleep. And you saw Stephan. Something like this might destroy him."

Catherine understood. April wanted Catherine to use her journalistic instincts to find her daughter.

It was not lost on Catherine how easily this might have been Catherine and Quentin, instead. They'd raised daughters. They understood.

"I'd be happy to look for her," Catherine agreed. "I'll do everything I can."

"We're happy to pay whatever you want," April assured her nervously.

"No," Catherine assured her. "This isn't about the money. It's about bringing a young woman back home."

In the back of her mind, Catherine understood that if she brought Felicity home, the family would be more apt to spill its secrets. Maybe Dee would even speak of Gwen —and what she'd hidden from the police seventy years ago.

But Catherine had to find Felicity first. It would be no easy feat.

Chapter Sixteen

It was two days since the incident at the beach. After a long and lackluster drive across the island, scouting for some sign of Nathan's sister and the other missing girls, Nathan and Scarlet were at the coffee shop. It was the same coffee shop where Scarlet had first spotted the hippie-dressed girls all those months ago. Nathan and Scarlet nibbled on blueberry croissants and watched the door quietly, almost as though they expected the girls to return and explain everything. A heaviness pressed across Scarlet's shoulders. She wasn't sure where to turn.

Nathan opened his laptop and scrolled through Reddit for additional information about the group. But it seemed like any information that popped up was immediately scrubbed a few minutes later. *They're doing everything they can to make sure they're not found.*

Scarlet wondered if Nathan regretted coming to Nantucket Island. It felt as though they'd hit a brick wall.

Scarlet opened her own laptop, connected to the

internet, and watched some of the footage Nathan had taken the other night. It was truly sensational stuff.

"It looks totally like a cult through the lens of this video," she breathed to Nathan.

"It looks totally like a cult, period," Nathan said.

Scarlet's stomach tied itself into knots. *We're in over our heads.*

Just then, there was a switch-over between shifts for the baristas. The young woman who'd been working the day Scarlet had seen the hippie girls entered with a tote bag slung over her shoulder. She frantically chewed a bright blue piece of gum and said to her coworker, "Josiah is *such an idiot.*"

Scarlet straightened her spine. Nathan gave her a curious look.

"We should interview her," Scarlet said. "She was here the day I was here. Maybe she's seen more of them?"

Nathan bobbed his head and got his camera out of his bag. Without talking about it, they both knew to wait to approach her until the other staff member left and the rest of the coffee shop was clear. Because it was a crystal-clear eighty-degree day, it didn't take long. Nobody wanted to be inside.

Nathan and Scarlet went up to the counter. Scarlet sensed how serious her smile was. The barista gave them a look that meant *what do you want?*

"Hey," Scarlet began, "we're working on a project. Would you be interested in helping?"

The barista shrugged. Scarlet spent a minute bumbling through her description of the hippie girls and asked, "Can you remember more times they came in here?"

Nathan was rolling. The barista stared into the

camera lens and chewed her gum. How old was she? Probably twenty-one or twenty-two? Probably the same age as most of the girls in that group?

Maybe her friends had been impacted.

"I guess I saw them?" the barista said. "But it's not a crime to, like, dress up."

Scarlet's heartbeat felt syncopated. "Did you get the sense that the girls were doing anything against their will?"

"No? I don't know. But it's not like people tell me *everything* on their mind when they come in here. And we get crazy busy."

"When was the last time they came in?" Scarlet asked. She was beginning to think this was another dead end.

"It must have been two weeks ago," the barista said. "It's always the same. The men wait outside, and the women get all the stuff and take it out to them. I thought maybe it was like a church. But you know, it's a free country. People practice all kinds of religions here."

Scarlet found it difficult not to show how disappointed she was.

But then it occurred to her.

This young woman had to work a summer job. She probably worked forty hours a week or more behind this very counter. It meant she didn't fit the mold of those other young women. *Her parents don't have wealth. Maybe her friends don't, either.*

She doesn't know anything else.

"Thanks for answering our questions," Scarlet said. "Have a great rest of your day."

Scarlet packed her stuff so quickly that Nathan had to scramble to keep up with her. They went outside. Scarlet collapsed into the driver's seat and pressed her forehead against her steering wheel. From the passenger seat, Nathan reached over and touched her shoulder.

"It's still early," he said softly.

"I'm just worried about them," Scarlet said.

She still wanted to go to the police. Nathan still refused.

"I don't want to miss our window," Scarlet said.

Nathan bowed his head. The air was taut.

That was when Scarlet got the idea to interview a ferry dock worker. She turned the key in the ignition and shot them out of the parking lot and back toward the harbor. Nathan thought it was a great idea.

"I'm sure they've seen them coming and going," he said, speaking quickly as he set up the camera again.

It took a little bit of probing at the docks, but they found someone willing and eager to talk about ten minutes into their search. The dock worker was in his sixties and was inexplicably missing an ear—a non-ferry-boat accident, he explained early on in the interview. It was clear he was tickled pink to be on camera.

"That's right," the dock worker said. "They came out in July or so. Must have been six weeks ago. A bunch of young women in long dresses and men in black shirts and pants."

"How many of them?" Scarlet asked.

"Maybe twenty women, twenty guys."

Scarlet looked at Nathan and thought, *They've added more since then.*

"Did you talk to them at all?" Scarlet asked.

The dock worker gave her a brash smile. "Sure did. It's not strange for me to talk to tourists. It's part of the reason I like the job so much. I asked them what they were up to in Nantucket. One of the guys looked at me like I was scum. Nobody was willing to answer anything real. The women were kind, but it was almost as though the guys were making sure they weren't talking much."

"Did you get the sense they weren't there of their own free will?" Scarlet asked.

"Not exactly, no." The dock worker removed a handkerchief from his pocket and dabbed his forehead. "I got the sense they weren't exactly thinking for themselves, but that isn't the same thing."

Scarlet searched her mind for another question, something else to enliven the interview. But the dock worker was already talking about other tourists he'd seen that summer—a man dressed in a lobster costume and a married couple who'd nearly thrown one another overboard.

"You see crazy stuff on this job," he said. "I'm the one to talk to about all that."

Scarlet thanked him and told Nathan to cut.

Back in Scarlet's car, they watched the footage and agreed it was pretty good although it offered no additional details.

It was nearly five thirty in the afternoon. Scarlet's stomach was empty and aching.

As though she'd sensed it, Grandma Greta sent a nudge of affection and an invitation for dinner. Scarlet pitched the idea to Nathan, who agreed wholeheartedly. It would be nice to get out of their heads for the night.

Scarlet parked in front of The Copperfield House and led Nathan into the kitchen, where Greta sliced onions and garlic and listened to classical music. Scarlet's eyes filled with tears—maybe because of the onions or perhaps because of how normal the scene was. Greta kissed her and said, "Welcome! Grab yourself a drink from the fridge if you'd like."

Scarlet and Nathan poured themselves sparkling lemonade and chatted to Greta for a little while about her day. Greta was giddy about a "breakthrough" she'd had in her novel.

Not long after that, Ivy and Quentin arrived. Ivy carried an apple pie they'd purchased from a farmers' market downtown. She set it gingerly on the counter.

Scarlet studied Ivy's face. Something was off about it. Sour. *Maybe she got into a fight with her boyfriend. Perhaps she's still brokenhearted about having to go back to university.*

Nathan tugged Scarlet's elbow and whispered in her ear. "Let's interview your sister before dinner."

Scarlet cocked her head with surprise. This was *her* project, and she hadn't wanted anyone in her family to know about it yet.

But Nathan pushed it. "She's the same age as the others. Maybe she's heard something?"

Scarlet heaved a sigh and slapped her hands across her thighs. Nathan was right.

"Ivy? Can you help us with something outside?" she asked.

Quentin and Greta were busy chatting about Bernard's new medication and what the doctor had said about how often to take it. It didn't sound serious; just another routine pill required when you got a little bit older.

The conversation meant they didn't notice Nathan, Ivy, and Scarlet slip out the door.

Nathan grabbed the camera as Scarlet selected choice

words for Ivy. She didn't want to tell Ivy absolutely everything. Not yet.

"A few girls around your age have left college recently," Scarlet began. "They've all joined this big group here in Nantucket." She was careful not to use the word "cult."

Ivy blinked dully at Scarlet. It was as though she hardly heard her.

"Have you heard anything about that? Like, is there any gossip going around?" Scarlet asked.

Nathan was already filming behind her. Ivy furrowed her brow.

"What's that?" she demanded.

"We're making a documentary," Scarlet said. "His little sister disappeared with this group, and we're trying to figure out why. What do they want? Will they ever leave? That kind of thing."

Ivy's nose twitched. A moment of silence passed. "I don't know anything about that."

Something tugged at Scarlet's consciousness. "But you went to high school with some of them," she said. "Haven't you seen anything on social media? Aren't people talking about it?"

Ivy shrugged. "Honestly, it isn't my business what people do with their time."

Scarlet was taken aback.

Then again, Ivy sounded much more sophisticated and adult than ever.

"Social media has rotted all of our minds," Ivy said. "It makes us think we're privy to information about each other's lives, even when people want to be private. Privacy is no longer respected. It's deemed *strange*. But it's a basic human right!"

Scarlet glanced back at Nathan, who continued to roll the camera. She slid her hand over her neck to cut. He did and grimaced.

"I'm sorry," Scarlet stuttered. "You're right."

Ivy swept her fingers through her long, glossy hair. She gave Scarlet a look Scarlet couldn't understand. "I have to get going," she said.

Scarlet felt it like a knife in her belly. "I'm really sorry, Ivy. I didn't mean to make you angry."

"It's whatever. I have plans anyway."

"With your boyfriend?" Scarlet asked.

Ivy nodded. "Yeah." She traipsed away from The Copperfield House and headed back toward the Nantucket Historic District.

Scarlet and Nathan remained on the lush grass outside of The Copperfield House. They watched her, confusion etched across their faces.

Chapter Seventeen

Catherine returned to Rainer, April, and Stephan's apartment in the Upper West Side that evening. The doorman gave her a grim hello and opened the door to the opulent lobby. "Mrs. Fellini is expecting you," he said.

Catherine thanked him. She entered and took the elevator all the way to the top.

This time, April hadn't bothered to make herself up for a visitor. Catherine knew the single worst fact of April's life—that her daughter was gone—and thus, the facade fell. Catherine had been among the affluent long enough to understand that every wealthy person built up a persona; that everything was false and apt to crack when times got tough. Catherine had experienced that herself when she'd been diagnosed with cancer. All her care about society and *what people thought* had gone out the window.

She'd focused on what mattered.

April wore a pair of pajama pants and a sweatshirt, and her hair hung in a loose ponytail. The only light in the house came from the television, where April watched reruns of *Gilmore Girls*. A shiver went down Catherine's spine. She loved watching that show with her girls. Probably, April did, too.

"Rainer and Stephan are visiting Dee," April explained as she led Catherine down the hall. Her hand shook when she opened the last door on the right.

Catherine understood that April didn't want her husband or her father-in-law to know she'd sought outside help. It was a matter of embarrassment.

Catherine and April stood in the middle of Felicity Fellini's bedroom. It was decorated in the style of a teenager-turned-twenty-one-year-old—with photographs of friends who changed from braces to long-legged models within the course of a couple of years, posters of pop stars, and handwritten lyrics and notes. It might have been Ivy or Scarlet's room.

"Rainer and I haven't been able to bring ourselves to go through her things," April said quietly. "It feels too invasive."

But the way she said it meant: *we need you to do it.*

"Would you like something to drink? Eat?" April asked as she backed out of the room. It was as though the place was haunted.

"I'm fine, thanks." Catherine set her jaw. She wanted to say something like *I'm going to find her.* But she knew better than to make promises she couldn't keep.

April clicked the door closed and left Catherine in Felicity's space. Catherine took a deep breath and searched her gut for her journalistic instincts. She needed them. *Why would a girl like Felicity skip out on her glorious life at the drop of a hat?*

But Catherine had been in the business long enough

to know that nothing like that really happened out of the blue. Something had happened. Felicity had met someone; she'd been clued into an idea about the world. Maybe there was a diary that would chart those events.

Catherine had brought gloves just in case. She hoped and prayed the room wouldn't require police investigation, but she didn't want to leave fingerprints if it did. She didn't want to mess anything up.

Catherine went through the desk first. She found diligent notes from Felicity's classes at Columbia, a printed-out application for an internship at a Midtown magazine set for the current summer, and several more photographs. She found books that Felicity had underlined and underlined, probably for a paper in an English class. But there was nothing like a diary in any of it.

Catherine kept going. She went under the bed, scooped through the clothes in a pile in the walk-in closet, and looked through the bedding. She searched for hiding places. She found several things Felicity had wanted to hide—including a photograph she'd taped on the underside of a drawer. The photograph was of Felicity and a handsome guy a couple of years older than her. The guy wore a black T-shirt and a black hat. Felicity wore a long dress that covered her arms and went all the way up her neck. Was that kind of thing back in style?

Something about the photo gave Catherine pause. She put it in a plastic ziplock bag, which she stored in her purse. Maybe she'd need to ask someone about the guy down the line. Maybe April would even know who he was.

Catherine sat on the edge of Felicity's bed and searched online for Felicity's social media. Of course, Felicity hadn't posted anything since right before she'd "disappeared." But her activity prior to her disappearance wasn't exactly normal. Alarm bells rang in Catherine's ears.

All the way through 2021, 2022, and most of 2023, Felicity seemed like a normal, healthy, happy teenage girl. She posted photos of her friends and song lyrics; she complained about school. She posted photos of her parents on vacation, one of Dee playing poker, and another of her entire family on a Mediterranean beach.

But by October of 2023, there was a sharp shift in Felicity's online presence. It was then she began posting things with quasi-intellectual slants. But most of the posts did not support feminist values. In fact, they seemed rather backward, in support of women abandoning the pursuit of education in pursuit of family.

Another of Felicity's posts read, "They want us to give them everything. Push, push, push yourself through every conceivable test and paper and class. For what? I've been working to get into a good university since I was eight years old. And now that I'm in one, I feel so empty. What is it all for?"

She was burned out, Catherine thought.

But it seemed Felicity had decided her burn-out was the fault of society. It seemed she wanted to return to old-fashioned values—and loosen herself from modern constraints.

Catherine had never seen anything like it.

Why would a young, intelligent woman—a woman with everything—fight her own principles like that? Why would a woman reject the hard work of generations of women before her?

It didn't make sense.

Catherine left Felicity's bedroom after two and a half

hours of searching. She found April in front of the television, wrapped in a ball. She gave Catherine a brief and hopeful smile that soon fell. It seemed April had expected Catherine to find her daughter within the span of a couple of hours.

"I made good progress," Catherine told her. She made sure to keep her voice formal. "I'll be in touch."

April didn't walk her to the elevator this time. Just before the elevator doors closed, Catherine heard April whimpering.

* * *

It was late—nearly eight, but Catherine decided to charge forth with her next plan of action. She'd transplanted her obsession with finding her grandfather with finding Felicity. *As long as I have something to obsess over, I'm happy,* she thought.

Based on last semester's syllabus Catherine had found in Felicity's room, Catherine wrote a few emails to Felicity's professors.

Dear Professors,

My name is Catherine Copperfield. I'm a freelance journalist, currently looking into the disappearance of Felicity Fellini. It is my understanding that she took your course last semester. I'm eager to speak with you if you have time.

Catherine didn't expect to hear back before the night was through. But ten minutes after she'd sent the emails, her phone dinged. It was a message from Professor Timothy Grass, Felicity's Creative Writing professor. Catherine bolted upright.

Dear Catherine Copperfield,

Yes. I'd be happy to talk. I'll be in my office at Columbia from eight to noon tomorrow morning. I look forward to seeing you there.

Professor Grass

Catherine could hardly sleep that night. She felt just as she had as a young and hungry reporter—so eager to tie up all the loose strands into a wild yet articulate story.

She woke up early for a run, then called Quentin as she drank coffee. He could hear the exhilaration in her voice.

"I can't wait to read this book!" he said because he still thought she was looking for Gionnocaro.

"It's gotten a whole lot weirder." That was all Catherine could bring herself to say.

Catherine reached the Department of Creative Writing at Columbia University by eight forty-five that morning. It was still August, and the students hadn't yet returned to campus, which gave the long and high ceilings a feeling of alienation. Just a few people milled about, walking too quickly, their steps echoing. Catherine walked quickly, too.

She reached Professor Grass's office and steeled herself before she knocked.

A kind voice called, "Come in!"

Catherine entered and found a man with a grizzled beard seated behind a desk. He wrote with an ornate pen and seemed to hide behind a pair of white eyebrows as thick as caterpillars.

Catherine fixed her face into a professional smile. But before she could say a thing, Professor Grass offered, "Catherine Copperfield, I presume?" He gestured toward the chair across from him.

Catherine bowed her head and closed the door

behind her. Despite the ninety-degree weather outside, it was surprisingly chilly in here. Goose bumps ran up her arms.

"You're looking for the Fellini girl," the professor stated, leaning back in his wooden chair until it creaked. "That was a mysterious event indeed."

Catherine took out a notebook for notes. "Can you tell me why it was so mysterious? From your perspective, I mean."

"I can really only tell any story from my perspective, unfortunately," the professor said.

Catherine offered a small smile.

"This wasn't the first time I had Felicity Fellini in class," Professor Grass began. She took Introduction to Creative Writing her freshman year and carried on with it sophomore year as well. I was struck by her writing. It was far more mature than the other students her age. But I could sense, too, that she pushed herself more than they did. She was very hard on herself. I don't think she always slept very well. She had big bags under her eyes."

"I suppose it's hard to keep up at Columbia sometimes," Catherine suggested, remembering the social media posts Felicity had made before her disappearance.

"Something was weighing on her," Professor Grass said. "My first hunch was familial pressure. Felicity's great-grandmother is the great Dee Fellini, and her great-grandfather came from Italian royalty. I believe the Fellinis always thought themselves better than everyone. And they needed their daughter to validate their beliefs."

Catherine was beginning to get the picture. *Too much pressure. A breakdown.*

"There's no easy way to say this," Professor Grass

said. "Felicity began dressing differently in February or March of last semester."

"Differently how?"

Professor Grass scratched the skin under his beard. "Long dresses. No skin exposed. The styles were vaguely hippie-ish, but with a sense of conservatism. Propriety. I wondered if she'd found religion or something. And it's really none of my business, you know. These kids enter university and experiment with all sorts of things. But a few weeks later, a man a couple of years older than her appeared outside the classroom door every day to walk her out. He was peculiar. He always addressed me head-on—as though nothing frightened him. Not that I'm a frightening man, but I do enjoy a sense of, shall we say, respect at Columbia. And this man did not respect me in the slightest."

Catherine squinted, then dug into her purse for the photograph of Felicity and the man dressed in black. She set the ziplock bag on the desk in front of Professor Grass. He adjusted his glasses and nodded.

"That's him," he said. "A boyfriend, I suppose? But something was very odd about it."

"What about her writing?" Catherine asked. "Did that take a turn, too?"

Professor Grass's eyes darkened. "Yes. Very much so. I remember she wrote a story about a very depressed young woman who dropped out of society and never spoke to anyone she'd ever known again. It worried me, especially with her startling personality change. I asked her to come to office hours, but she didn't." He sniffed. "It was a well-written story. It felt terribly real."

Catherine knew these were all clues. But they were

the sort of clues that didn't necessarily add up to anything. She couldn't give them too much power.

"A few other young women started dressing like that last semester, too," Professor Grass finished. "It was bizarre. Truly bizarre. But I decided at the time it was just another trend. That's what the kids do, you know. They fall into trends. They let themselves get swept up."

Catherine jotted several additional notes to herself, then glanced up. Professor Grass gazed out the window thoughtfully. It was as though he was in another dimension.

"Thank you for your help, Professor," Catherine said quietly.

"Any time," Professor Grass said. "I hope it's all a misunderstanding. I hope she's safe."

It was all the rest of them could do right now—*hope*.

But Catherine still had a job to do.

Chapter Eighteen

Scarlet and Nathan spent every day out of doors, scouring the island, working on the documentary. Later tonight, they had plans to watch the "cult" from a distance as the sun burst in pinks and yellows behind them and the bonfire shimmered along the sand.

This afternoon, they interviewed a married couple on the island who'd lost their daughter recently—presumably to the same group they were after. Nathan had discovered their post on Reddit, pleading with the community for information about where their daughter might have gone. Nathan and Scarlet had set up their camera in the well-tended living room of the mini-mansion in Siasconset and asked questions of the parents. *When was the last time you heard from your daughter? How old is she? Did she mention any men? Did you get the sense she was dating them? Did her style change before you last saw her?*

The parents were mystified. They'd sent their daughter money but demanded she come home; they'd said they would stop sending money if she didn't. But still, they worried, and they sent more money along. *How could they not? They loved her so much. They wanted her to be safe.*

"Thank you for talking to us today," Scarlet said as she cut the camera.

The mother rubbed her temples and glanced at her husband. "We've been too embarrassed to say anything. But we realized it's better to say something than never see her again."

Nathan tucked the camera into his bag. "My sister disappeared, too."

Scarlet was surprised that he confessed this.

The mother gasped. "How is your mother handling it?"

"She won't talk about it," Nathan admitted.

The father wrapped his arm around his wife's shoulders and held her close. He eyed the camera, Scarlet, and their car outside.

"We don't know what they're up to," Nathan said. "But we think they're close."

The husband gasped. "In Nantucket?"

Scarlet squeezed Nathan's arm. She didn't want them to make a fuss or contact the police until they knew more. *We can't let them slip away.*

"We're not sure," Nathan said. "But we're on the verge of breaking it wide open. We'll have enough to get the girls out of there. I'm sure of it."

Scarlet was surprised at how open and honest he sounded—especially because much of what he said was a lie.

I wonder if he's lied to me, Scarlet wondered, then shivered.

They left the mini-mansion. It was nearly six, and the air was different, tinged with orange and smelling of grills and bonfires. Scarlet imagined hundreds of families across the island, showering the sand away, preparing for dinner. She imagined mothers ordering their children to wash their hands and set the table.

She thought of her own mother, whom she hadn't heard from since she'd left New York City. Because Nathan was driving, she sent a text.

> SCARLET: I miss you. I hope your work is going well.

Catherine didn't write back right away.

Nathan pulled into a gas station about a mile away from town. Scarlet's car was on empty, and they wanted to get snacks for their stakeout later. They'd resolved to park at a greater distance than before so as not to draw attention to themselves.

"What kind of snacks do you want?" Scarlet asked, clambering from the passenger seat and stretching her arms over her head. "Twizzlers? Doritos?"

Nathan removed the nozzle from the tank and slipped it into the gas notch on the opposite side of the car. "Twizzlers, yes. Doritos? Too messy."

Scarlet giggled. They'd fallen into a nice routine together, one demanded of people who didn't know each other well and who'd been forced into proximity.

One day, I walked into a cinema in Greenwich Village, and my entire life changed, she imagined telling someone one day. But then again, it wasn't like she and Nathan had even kissed—except for that very first time.

It wasn't that she didn't think about it.

But they had so many other things to fight for.

And the fact that they still weren't any closer to

figuring out where the girls were staying was frustrating for them both.

Especially for him, she knew. This was his sister. He was terribly worried.

And he wanted to make his parents proud.

Suddenly, a station wagon pulled into the gas station and buzzed to a stop at the gas tank farthest from them. Scarlet hardly glanced at it.

"I'll pick something else out," Scarlet said after a pause. "Twizzlers and a surprise snack."

"Great." Nathan offered a sad, tired, sunburnt smile and continued putting gas in the tank.

Scarlet headed for the glass door of the gas station and entered the air-conditioned chill. She grabbed a couple of beers for later, plus some diet soda and Twizzlers.

When she was perusing the chips, her eyes lifted, and she peered across the aisles and through the dirty, streaked windows.

The man who'd gotten out of the station wagon wore all black.

Scarlet froze with panic. *People wear black all the time,* she reminded herself. *It might not be anything.*

Scarlet crept to the counter with her snacks and spread them out. Nathan was done putting gas in the tank and had returned to the driver's side, where he tapped his hands on the steering wheel and sang along to the song on the radio.

The gas station employee returned from breaking down boxes to scan Scarlet's items. The man in black strode inside and flashed a hand to the employee before disappearing behind the aisle of peanuts and beef jerky.

Scarlet couldn't breathe. *Is he in the cult?*

"You having a good one?" the gas station employee asked Scarlet.

"Sure thing. You?" Scarlet's voice shook.

Scarlet paid for the gas and the items and gathered the plastic bag. She could feel the man in black behind her; he was like a black cloud.

"How you doing, Bobby?" the man in black asked the employee. It was clear he'd been here several times before.

"Not bad, Kid." The attendant looked at Scarlet in a way that said she'd been standing there too long.

Scarlet forced a smile and said, "Night!" then stepped into the muggy evening. Being as casual as she could, she turned on a dime and headed for the trash can near the station wagon. She wanted to see inside.

Once there, she shelled her things of its plastic bag and glanced into the back seat of the station wagon. Sure enough, there they were: three young women. Their hair was long and wavy; their eyes were straight ahead. They looked as though they'd time-traveled from another era.

One of them was Ivy's friend from high school. The original one she'd seen that day at the coffee shop.

I should run over there, throw open the station wagon door, and tell them to come with me.

But what about the others?

Scarlet's tongue felt thick, as though she'd bitten it. She hurried back to her car and got inside as delicately as she could.

"What did you decide on?" Nathan asked, turning the music down. He prepared to start the engine.

Scarlet kept her eyes straight ahead and said, "They're in that station wagon."

The air in the car crystallized. Nathan sat up straight.

"Don't make any false moves," she ordered. "We don't want them to think we're onto them."

"They just come to the gas station like this? Out in the open?"

"They're not doing anything illegal," Scarlet reminded him.

"That we know of," Nathan spat.

They remained quiet. The man left the gas station, whistling to himself, and got into the station wagon. Once there, he revved the engine and crept out.

"I want to follow them," Nathan muttered.

Scarlet inhaled sharply. She was terrified. But this was the only way.

We have to find out where they live.

"Just be careful," Scarlet said. She guessed Nathan had never stalked anyone before. But then again, what did she know about him, really? *What does anyone know about the first person they kissed?*

"Get the camera," Nathan muttered as he crept out of the gas station parking lot and turned right, following the station wagon from a great distance.

Scarlet hurried to pull the camera out of its case. She set up a messy shot of the road, then turned to record Nathan, his hands firm at the steering wheel.

Nathan narrated for a bit. "We just had a fortuitous encounter. We're after them, following at a comfortable distance. We don't want them to get the idea we're following them. But they're going to lead us right to their lair."

Scarlet laughed, although it sounded strange and sinister. "Lair is a good word," she said.

Nathan chuckled, too. They were jittery and wild.

They drove in silence after that. Scarlet kept the

camera pinned to the station wagon, which was a good quarter of a mile ahead of them. They were driving the speed limit, presumably because they didn't want to get pulled over.

Scarlet wondered, *What happens when we find the house? Do we storm in and get everyone out? What if they don't want to go? Do we ask them why?*

Documentary making was an art form. It was also fast and loose, apt to change at a moment's notice. She had no idea what would happen next—in life or in the movie.

Suddenly, the station wagon bucked off the main road and down a ditch. Scarlet let out a cry of alarm.

"Where are they going?"

"We're going to find out," Nathan said darkly.

"We can't go down that ditch—" Scarlet began.

But already, Nathan twisted the tires and charged after the station wagon down a little side road that took them into a shadowy forest. Scarlet reached over and squeezed Nathan's wrist.

"They'll see us coming," she breathed.

Nathan's forehead bubbled with sweat. He cut the engine and exhaled. He knew she was right.

"Let's follow the road on foot," he suggested.

"We have to move the car," she said.

Nathan grimaced. He revved the engine and reversed up the ditch and onto the road. He then drove up five hundred feet, put on the blinkers, and cut the engine again. Scarlet's stomach ached. She wasn't sure what they were getting themselves into. She reached into the back seat and removed a baseball bat she kept back there—just in case.

Nathan gave her a firm nod. They had to keep going.

Nathan and Scarlet walked through the shadows of

the thick woods. Neither of them spoke. But Scarlet's mind was awash with thoughts like *I was raised in the city! I wasn't meant for this!*

We're going to figure out what they're up to. We're going to save them.

What if they capture us, and we never see the light of day again?

Throughout, Nathan filmed the walk carefully. "We'll want the footage," he promised.

Scarlet knew he was right. Again, she felt grateful for the power he lent every situation.

Fifteen minutes later, the trees cleared, and they could make out a fifteen-foot fence that surrounded what looked to be several acres. It was difficult to make out what was on the other side. Scarlet squeezed Nathan's hand. She was terrified.

"What are they doing back there?" she breathed.

Nathan set his jaw.

Together, they stared at the locked gate. It was not clear what they would do next. But Scarlet took the camera and filmed all she could.

Chapter Nineteen

Catherine pulled her car into the belly of the ferry that night at seven, cut the engine, and got out to stretch her legs on the top deck. It had felt like a terribly long drive from Manhattan. Her mind was crowded with fears and questions about Felicity Fellini, as well as Gionnocaro Fellini—both of them—and her grandma Gwen. It had been difficult to keep her mind on the road, her hands at ten and two. Her heart was elsewhere.

She was forty-eight years old. And it was increasingly clear that she knew less about the world now than ever—if only because she was aware of just how diverse and strange the world really was.

Catherine leaned against the ferry railing and watched the island come closer on the dark horizon. Quentin was in Martha's Vineyard, tending to another documentary project, and said he wouldn't be back till later. But Catherine wanted to make a pit stop at The Copperfield House anyway. She'd learned via the Copperfield group chat that most of the family was over for dinner. Catherine wanted to slip into the Copperfield family's boisterous laughter and funny stories; she wanted to eat divine food, drink a glass of wine with Greta, and forget the pains of the day.

That was when she realized Scarlet had texted her earlier today. Catherine was so out of her mind that things like that were slipping through the cracks.

CATHERINE: I'm back now!

CATHERINE: Are you coming to The Copperfield House for dinner?

But Scarlet didn't answer right away. And soon, it was time for Catherine to return to her vehicle.

Catherine drove immediately to The Copperfield House, parked on the road, and got out. A few of the Copperfield grandchildren raced across the sands. Alana and Julia wore cutoffs and flipped through magazines on the steps of the back porch.

Ivy was in the middle of them, coming closer, kicking her feet through the sand. Catherine's heart thudded. Here she was: her beautiful middle child, who would return to New York University soon. Catherine had missed too much of her time at home. She cursed herself and promised herself she'd go to the city often to make it up to Ivy—and herself.

You blink, and your children are grown.

Catherine hurried to scoop Ivy into a hug. Ivy offered a soft smile.

"How was the city?" Ivy asked, peeling herself from her mother.

"It was interesting," Catherine answered.

Ivy didn't ask any additional questions. She flipped her hair and turned her head.

Catherine's stomach felt like it was eating herself. She'd find a way to talk to Ivy as soon as she grabbed a snack.

Catherine led Ivy inside to find Greta at the kitchen stove as always. Ivy grabbed a glass of water and returned to the beach, where she slung herself across a towel and read a novel. *Okay, I'll talk to her later,* Catherine decided as she nibbled on a piece of cheese.

"Is Ivy doing all right?" Catherine asked.

"She's seemed particularly thoughtful lately," Greta answered as she unfurled a carrot from its skin. "I'm sure it's just about school. I was always worried about school at her age. I was always worried I wouldn't get to where I wanted to be."

"You were the most driven woman at the Sorbonne," Ella said as she entered with a platter of fresh bread.

"She was the most driven *person* at the Sorbonne," Bernard said, entering the kitchen briefly to give Greta a kiss on the cheek. "Gender had nothing to do with it." Bernard took a slice of gouda and winked at Catherine, then said, "How was the city?"

Catherine smiled. "Messy."

Greta laughed knowingly. "It always is."

"My wife tells me you're up to your elbows in stories," Bernard said. "I hope you'll regale us with a few when we sit down for dinner."

"You know how she is," Greta reminded him. "She's just like our son. She keeps it all locked away until it's ready."

Catherine's heart swelled with the sudden desire to

see Quentin as soon as possible. She couldn't wait till he got home tonight. She couldn't wait to cuddle him close.

"But it has to do with your grandfather, correct?" Bernard pushed it.

"It did," Catherine said.

"Past tense!" Bernard raised his eyebrows.

"Like I said. Things got messy," Catherine said.

They sat for dinner at eight thirty. Catherine sat between her children James and Ivy and across from her sister-in-law Julia. She heaped butter chicken on her plate and listened to James's stories from a pickup baseball game that afternoon. The animation in his eyes made it difficult to believe he'd spent the majority of his life in the city rather than wild and free on an island.

Midway through dinner, Ivy scooted her chair back. She'd been very quiet, only saying please and thank you as the food was passed around. There were dark shadows beneath her eyes.

Catherine was suddenly terrified that Ivy wasn't eating enough. It had happened to Alana's stepdaughter, Sarah. Why not Ivy, too?

Ivy twisted to look at Catherine. "May I be excused?"

Catherine was caught off guard. Ivy's voice was sweet and sincere; her plate was clean. It might have been any other normal night. But something about this gave Catherine pause.

"Where are you off to?" Catherine asked.

"I'm meeting some friends," Ivy said.

Catherine's stomach thundered. "Which friends?"

"Just some island friends. You don't know them," Ivy told her.

Catherine wiped her mouth with a linen napkin. She

reminded herself, *Ivy goes to college. She's accustomed to doing what she wants.*

"Okay. Let me know if you need someone to pick you up later," she said.

"Yeah. Cool." Ivy went around the table to kiss Greta and give Bernard a high-five. "Have a good night, guys!"

With that, Ivy rushed out into the night, disappearing on the other side of the house. Next came the sound of the engine of her car.

Never should have gotten her a car, Catherine thought glumly.

After dinner, Catherine washed dishes in the kitchen while Alana and Julia dried and put them away. Greta was at the kitchen table with a glass of Malbec. Catherine's mind was still heavy with thoughts of Ivy. Finally, she turned and looked Greta in the eye.

"Have any of you seen Ivy's boyfriend?"

Greta smiled and set down her glass. "I haven't seen him, no. But I heard he's handsome."

"Who said that?" Alana asked.

"One of the girls was saying so. Was it Laura?" Greta furrowed her brow.

Catherine scrubbed another plate. "I hope she doesn't want to go long distance with him after she returns to school."

"Why not?" Greta asked. "Long distance is romantic."

How could Catherine answer? *Because Ivy needs to be focused on school. She can't throw herself totally into her romantic relationship. She can't get lost in it before she even knows who she is.*

The front door screamed open, and Scarlet appeared in the kitchen a moment later. She looked glum and tired.

Greta wrapped her in a hug, and Catherine dried her hands and did the same.

"Where were you?" Greta demanded. "Oh, but don't worry. We have plenty of leftovers." She returned to the kitchen table, then added, "Where's your friend?"

"He's back home," Scarlet said. "Too tired to come out."

But there was a flicker of something in Scarlet's eyes when she said that. Catherine had the sudden and inexplicable hunch that Scarlet was *lying about something.*

But what would she lie about? About the guy?

"We were just talking about Ivy's boyfriend," Catherine said. "He's such a mystery."

Scarlet nodded as she piled a plate with butter chicken and put it in the microwave. "She really likes him."

"Have you met him?" Greta asked.

"Nope." Scarlet looked downtrodden. She sat across from her grandmother.

What's going on? Catherine wondered.

Suddenly, she wanted to draw Scarlet deeper into her world. She wanted to tell her everything she'd learned about Gionnocaro the first and second; everything Dee had said at the nursing home; everything she suspected of Felicity Fellini.

But she also didn't want to frighten Scarlet. Whatever these people were up to, it wasn't kind or nice or good. She wanted to protect her.

Not long after she ate, Scarlet left The Copperfield House, promising she'd be back soon. Catherine packed up, too, and drove James back home. He fell asleep in the passenger seat even though the drive was only ten minutes long. Catherine's heart swelled.

Quentin got home just a few minutes after they did. Catherine leaped on him joyfully and covered him with kisses. He was boisterous with stories, and Catherine was allowed to forget her own for a little while. They went into the bedroom and lay down, holding hands. Catherine wondered if Quentin would want to do a documentary about the Fellini girl and whatever happened to her. Maybe he'd want to do a documentary about Gionnocaro Fellini—the first and second.

Maybe they could even work together for the first time in years.

Catherine and Quentin fell asleep a little past midnight. Catherine waded through dreams and night-mares, tossing and turning.

But when the gray light of the morning streamed through the bedroom window, Catherine was up and ready for her run.

She raced downstairs, stretching out her legs and arms. She drank water and peered out at the thrashing water, proof that the weather had turned sometime last night.

Then, without thinking about it, Catherine went to the garage to make sure Ivy's car was there.

She opened the door and stood in the doorway, staring at where Ivy's car was always parked—between James's and Quentin's. Her heart slowed to a stop. Her knees clacked together.

Maybe she parked out front?

Catherine shot through the garage and peered down the road from left to right. Raindrops splattered her face. "Ivy?" she called, although she knew that was foolish of her. "Ivy?" she tried again.

Catherine's hands shook. She called Ivy's number,

but it went immediately to voicemail. Catherine called three more times before she bucked up the stairs to wake up Quentin.

She hasn't called. She hasn't texted. Something must have happened. Something the police don't know about yet.

Was this one of those terrible moments in life parents dread?

Was it happening to her?

Just before she reached the bedroom door, her phone lit up with a text from Ivy. Catherine exhaled all the air from her lungs.

IVY: Don't freak out. I'm okay.

IVY: But I'm not going back to college this year.

IVY: And I'm not coming home.

IVY: Don't try to find me.

Chapter Twenty

Scarlet woke up to the phone call from her mother. Blurry-eyed, she pressed the phone to her ear and heard, "Is she with you? Is Ivy with you?"

In the pit of her stomach, Scarlet already knew.

Scarlet scrambled out of bed and burst out the door and into the hall. Her mother was talking too fast; she couldn't make sense of it. She could hear her father in the background, his voice booming. He used several swear words. It was rare that he cursed.

"I need you to come over right now," Catherine ordered.

Scarlet's heart skipped a beat. *This can't be happening,* she thought.

That was when she remembered how long Ivy's hair was getting.

That was when she remembered how cagey Ivy was about her boyfriend.

Scarlet fell to the ground outside Nathan's bedroom. The world spun.

"Did you hear me, honey?" Catherine demanded. "Get in the car and come here right now!"

Catherine's reaction was a typical human reaction. She was frightened, and it came out as anger. Scarlet's was the same.

Already, tears drained from her eyes and stained her shirt.

Nathan's door burst open. In her ear, Catherine continued to cry. But Scarlet found herself safe in Nathan's arms. He held her as though he already understood. Maybe a part of him had always expected Ivy would be taken, too. Or perhaps he could already read her mind.

Maybe the first person you kiss can always read your mind, Scarlet thought. Then she chided herself for being so dumb.

"I'll be there soon," Scarlet told her mother. "I love you. It's going to be okay."

She hung up and blinked up at Nathan's face. She bit her tongue to keep from sobbing.

"Come on," Nathan said. He hauled her to her feet and helped her to the kitchen, where he brewed a pot of coffee. "We know more than your mother does. We know where they are."

Scarlet stared into the black coffee and remembered yesterday how they'd crept down the trail to the fence that kept them out of the massive house just beyond; how they'd waited as long as they could until the sun began to set; how they'd raced out to their car and kept watch near the beach, where the same people had built a bonfire, and men had given speeches, and women had danced. In fact, it looked a little like a party. But Scarlet was sure their ideologies were backward. She was sure the women were being brainwashed. Maybe the men were, too.

Now, her sister was probably at that house in the woods.

Was she wearing one of those horrible hippie dresses? Was she acting like those other young women—as though she hadn't a single original thought in her head?

Nathan collected the film equipment and the computer with all the footage on it. They planned to show everything to Catherine and Quentin. Maybe they always should have done that. But Scarlet had wanted to craft her very first documentary by herself.

She was in over her head.

Nathan drove Scarlet to the house Quentin and Catherine had purchased last year; the house with the room painted lilac that Ivy and Scarlet shared when they were both home. Nathan carried everything inside and hung back while Scarlet hugged her parents and little brother. James, especially, was despondent. He'd probably heard Catherine and Quentin crying and yelling. It had affected him.

Nathan shook hands with Quentin and Catherine.

Scarlet thought, *He'll probably never be my boyfriend now.*

And then she wondered, *Did I really want him to be my boyfriend?* She wasn't sure anymore.

Scarlet had invited Nathan to The Copperfield House last night after they'd left the beach. But he'd been too despondent. "I can't pretend I'm happy in front of your grandmother," he'd explained. "I don't want them to think I'm this boring, lifeless guy just because I'm so upset about my sister."

Now, they would understand.

Nathan and Scarlet sat down with Quentin and Catherine at the kitchen table with cups of coffee. Quentin's eyes were rimmed with red.

At first, Catherine tried to start. "I've been researching these people," she explained. "They took a young woman from Manhattan. Felicity Fellini."

Scarlet tilted her head. "She must be related to us? Through Great-Grandpa?"

Catherine flinched. It seemed like a difficult question although Scarlet couldn't fathom why.

Scarlet explained the backstory. She'd seen the young women in the dresses earlier this summer and decided she wanted to create a documentary.

"That's how I met up with Nathan. It turns out his sister left with them, too," Scarlet explained timidly.

Nathan stared at the ground.

"Oh, Nathan." Catherine shook her head and cupped her coffee mug with both hands. "When did she leave?"

"Before the end of the spring semester," he explained. "My parents don't know what to do with themselves. But they absolutely won't talk about it."

"That was my experience, too," Catherine said. "The mother who asked me to look for her daughter waited until the last possible second to bring it up. I suspect that her husband didn't approve."

"It's all about appearances," Nathan agreed with a sigh.

Scarlet pulled her computer from her bag and set it on the table between them. "We've taken a lot of footage. Here."

Scarlet showed bits and pieces of everything they had so far: the interview with the parents and the dock worker; the video of the man in black who'd smacked the front window of her car; the bonfires; and their following them to the fenced-in mansion where, it seemed, they were all staying.

Scarlet watched her mother's face as she watched. She was captivated.

When it was over, Catherine looked Scarlet in the eye. It was clear she was proud of her. It was clear, too, that she was terrified.

"I wish you'd have told me about this sooner," Catherine offered.

"I wanted to do it on my own," Scarlet said.

"She's like us," Quentin said quietly, smacking his thighs.

Catherine wet her lips. "We have to be careful. We can't let them know how much we already know."

"That's what Nathan said," Scarlet remembered.

"Good instincts," Quentin said.

"I have a few ideas," Catherine said. Her eyes were stormy. "But I have a lot of work to do."

Scarlet saluted her mother. "Let us know what we can do."

It was remarkable how determined her mother was to survive and succeed. That translated easily to her love of her children—and her desire to keep them safe.

"We're going to find her," Catherine affirmed, then turned to look at Nathan. "We're going to find them both."

Chapter Twenty-One

Catherine urged Scarlet not to act rashly, not now that they knew Ivy was gone. Whoever these people were, they were dangerous and powerful enough to rip through the Copperfield family. Scarlet's eyes flashed with anger. She promised she'd keep herself at bay.

Catherine waffled between pride for Scarlet's purposeful decision to make a documentary on her own and irritation that Scarlet hadn't let her in. *But I didn't let her in, either,* Catherine reminded herself, watching as Scarlet packed up that morning and laced her fingers through Nathan's. Catherine had suggested they go for a long walk and clear their heads.

"If everything goes to plan, we'll have a lot on our plate the next few days," Catherine assured them. "And you'll have plenty of filming to do for the documentary."

Scarlet looked too tired to fight. She hugged her mother a final time, and Catherine felt as though a powerful fist was squeezing her heart.

After Scarlet and Nathan drove away, Catherine

burrowed her face into Quentin's chest and tried to re-direct her thoughts. A strategy stitched its way through her mind. But she had to act quickly and appeal to a sensibility she didn't fully understand, even after living as Quentin's wife for so long.

How to force the wealthy to do something. How to ask them to stop being so prideful—and pay attention.

Catherine made James a stack of pancakes as thick as a dictionary and escaped into her study upstairs. Quentin called up, saying, "Let me know if you need *anything*," and Catherine knew he meant it. And it was true that his face, his name, his voice would surely be instrumental in looping more of the parents of the girls into her plan.

But first, Catherine called April Fellini.

As the phone rang out from Nantucket to Manhattan, it occurred to Catherine she'd begun to think of April as an extended family member.

I wonder if I'll ever learn the connection between my Gionnocaro and theirs. But right now, it didn't matter. All she wanted was to bring their daughters home.

"Catherine?" April sounded stricken.

"Hi." Catherine pressed the heel of her hand against her forehead and gazed out the window at the white-tinged surf. "I wanted to let you know. My daughter was taken, too."

April gasped. She had no other words.

"But we know where they are," Catherine said. "My other daughter tracked them down."

April's breathing was chaotic and all over the place. But Catherine knew she listened as Catherine enlisted her for what she hoped would be tomorrow night's plan.

"But you have to be very, very cagey about this," Catherine said. "You cannot write anything on social media. We cannot spook them or chase them off the island. Everything is really delicate. Remember, as far as we know, they haven't broken the law. We just have to appeal to their sense of family; of memory; of time."

Catherine closed her eyes and remembered what Greta had told her; that memory was slippery and stories were always apt to change.

That history was always fiction.

April's voice shifted to a deeper tone. "I'm ready," she affirmed. "I'll pack a bag right away."

Catherine flared her nostrils. "We need to find as many parents as we can. I have a couple of other contacts —including myself and my husband. But we need more."

April was quiet. Catherine felt she could hear the ticking of her thoughts.

"You want me to call around?" April suggested after a pause.

"I know people don't want to confess that this has happened to them. I know people are embarrassed," Catherine breathed. "Especially the Manhattan elite. But if you, April, and me—Quentin Copperfield's wife—call around, maybe we'll make some headway."

"Quentin Copperfield's wife," April breathed with surprise.

"That's right." Catherine raised her chin. She was so many things; she had so many titles. But one of her most important ones was being his wife. She refused to lie about it now.

It gave her power in this world.

April agreed to call as many people as she could. Catherine thanked her and hung up. Her head throbbed, but she was filled with purpose. Scarlet's footage had done what every brilliant documentary was meant to do.

It had enlivened her. It had forced her to reckon with evils in the world—and enact change.

Of course, it was far more personal now that Ivy was involved. But still. Scarlet's footage had power.

Catherine spent all morning and afternoon calling the Manhattan elite. She rang Ivy's old friends' parents, Scarlet's old friends' parents, people she'd worked with during after-school bake sales and fundraisers, and the parents of those who'd taken piano lessons with Scarlet's teacher what felt like a million years ago. The first few parents suggested that Catherine was crazy for her questions, but the fourth mother burst into tears and confessed, "My friend Molly's daughter left, too. She says she's fine and keeps in contact, but she asks for more and more money and refuses to come home. They don't know where she is."

Catherine gently asked for Molly's contacts.

And before the hour was through, she had another three sets of parents—all of whom had connected with Molly via another channel.

Their group was growing.

Catherine called Scarlet late afternoon to confirm that Nathan's parents were coming, too.

"We alerted the parents we interviewed, too," Scarlet said. Her voice was brash and confident, like that of a documentarian rather than a frightened older sister. "They're ready."

She's going to be somebody, Catherine thought. *She can bring people together.*

Catherine thanked her daughter and left her study for the first time all day. Her stomach groaned with hunger, but she had no interest in slowing down. She grabbed a sweatshirt and her car keys and fled, headed for the police station. Although she reckoned they couldn't do much, she wanted to know what they already knew.

It turned out, they hardly knew anything at all.

Catherine found herself at the edge of her seat across from a bumbling police officer who was sunburnt from yesterday's fishing expedition. When she mentioned a big house in the woods with a fence around it, he laughed and said, "Which one? People like their privacy around here."

He wasn't taking her seriously.

Catherine then mentioned the massive bonfires and the young women in long dresses with the men who seemed to have power over them. But when the cop asked if the women were taken against their will, Catherine said no. He rolled his eyes.

"These young women are all between the ages of nineteen and twenty-three, you said?"

Catherine nodded.

"They're adults," he said. "They can do what they want. And their parents are funding them!"

Catherine's heart cracked at the edges. She set her jaw, sure she didn't want to show him how upset she was.

"We're going to stage a small protest tomorrow," Catherine told him. "And it is in my right to request police presence for safety reasons."

The police officer looked exhausted. His eyes glinted, as though he were sick and needed a twelve-hour night of sleep.

"Yes. It is in your right." He sighed and picked up a pen. "When do you need us?"

"Tomorrow night right before sunset," she said. "At Miacomet Beach."

The police exhaled deeply and jotted it down. "Fine.

Yes." He dropped the pen to the desk with a clatter. "We'll be there with bells on."

"I appreciate it."

* * *

Catherine was jittery the rest of the night. Quentin tried to get her to come to bed. He begged her and made her cups of tea. But all Catherine could do was sit on the edge of the sofa, half-watching mindless television and praying that tomorrow would go as planned. If she didn't, at least the protest would give them more information. But if it didn't, the group would surely leave Nantucket, and their trail might go cold.

"I don't have time for this," Catherine muttered.

She was suddenly terrified that the rest of the year would be consumed with following around these foolish young people. *Young people who thought they knew more about the world than their elders. Young people who'd decided to make up their own rules.*

Catherine wanted to sit with Ivy in a quiet room and ask her, *Why? Why did you leave? Why did you trust them?*

But in order to ask those questions, she needed Ivy safe and at home.

Catherine, Quentin, and James met Scarlet and Nathan and Nathan's parents at the beach next to where the group met for bonfires and late-night celebrations. Nathan's parents were volatile, speaking in low tones to each other and often bickering. They shook Quentin's and Catherine's hands, their eyes traveling up Quentin's body. Although they were distracted, they still couldn't get over the fact that *Quentin Copperfield was really here.*

"My daughter used to be quite impressed by you," Nathan's father said. "Maybe your presence will knock some sense into her."

Nathan's mother squeezed Nathan's father's elbow hard until he winced.

Catherine rubbed Scarlet's upper back as they waited for the other parents to come. Catherine had dropped a pin via their group chat to tell them where they would be. Parents had taken days off work; they'd called in sick; they'd brought their other children to grandparents and friends. Slowly, luxury vehicle after luxury vehicle parked along the edge of the beach. Catherine had told them to park separate from one another, just in case one of the group members drove along and saw too many vehicles together.

Scarlet gave Catherine a look that meant, *I can't believe this is happening.*

But very soon, there were more than thirty-five people in their group. Parents had reached out to other parents; wealthy people had confessed that their daughters had gone.

April and Rainer Gionnocar came not long after that. Catherine's heart leaped into her throat. *I'm not related to them,* she reminded herself. *But why does it feel like I've known them all my life?*

Catherine hurried over and threw her arms around April's shoulders. April shook like a frightened bird. Rainer looked discombobulated. As he took a call, April muttered, "His grandmother Dee told him to brush off his pride and come to Nantucket."

Catherine remembered the fire in that older woman's eyes. "She's really something."

April tilted her head. "Sometimes it feels bizarre to

me that I married into this wealthy family. And then I remember Dee. She came from nothing, too."

"Like me," Catherine admitted.

"Maybe none of us really come from anything," April suggested. "Gionnocaro Fellini supposedly came from royalty. But what do any of us really know about his past?"

"It could all be pretend," Catherine agreed.

Just before they began their march to the opposite beach, the other Copperfields arrived: Greta and Bernard and Alana and Jeremy; Julia and Charlie; Ella and Will. Catherine hugged them with her eyes closed, listening to the burgeoning beats of their hearts.

There's so much love here, she thought.

It was nearly time. The police were here, guiding their group from one beach to another. They wore bemused expressions.

Scarlet and Catherine linked arms and led the charge of fifty-plus parents and brothers and sisters and friends to the bonfire that surged in the distance. Catherine squinted to make out a man in black, his arms spread as he spoke his "wisdom" to the crowd of young women and men beneath him.

His voice echoed from the water, and Catherine could just make out what he said, "It's the pressure of modern society. It's an endless machine that we must feed and feed and feed. And for what? What if we gave up on all of that? What if we just stopped what they wanted us to do—and lived for ourselves?"

Catherine took a sharp breath. She partially agreed with what the young man was saying. There simply *was* too much pressure on young people today—especially women. Now that women were allowed to live and work outside the home, and they could carve lives for them-selves, they were expected to do *absolutely everything.* They had to cook and clean and tend to their children; they had to make as much money as men; they had to fill their lives with impossible tasks. It was enough to make anyone feel insane—and underappreciated.

But there had to be a better way than stepping out from society. This act of departure was just as juvenile as the hippie culture of the sixties and seventies.

We have to get better as a society. We have to find a way together.

Suddenly, the young man making the speech stopped talking. He'd seen the crowd approaching with police. He raised both of his hands. All the people who'd been listening to him turned around and gaped. Catherine searched them for Ivy but saw only beautiful, youthful faces she didn't recognize.

The man who'd been giving the speech raised his hands and called out, "We are peaceful! We have done nothing illegal! There's no reason for police presence!"

Catherine brought her hands around her mouth to call back, "This is a peaceful protest! But we have a right to have police presence!"

Catherine's voice rang out across the beach. *Do you hear me, Ivy? Do you know how much I love you?*

Children never really know, Catherine knew. Not until they have children of their own.

The group of parents was now only fifteen feet from the crowd around the bonfire. The man wearing black was muttering something to the people around him, some-thing that sounded like, "Stay calm. Stay strong. We know what we're all about. We know we won't go back."

But just then, a father stepped out from the crowd.

Quietly, he said, "Melanie?" His voice was tender, searching. "Melanie, we just want you to come home. We don't want anything else. We love you."

The air was taut.

Then a young woman Catherine recognized from Ivy's school days burst into tears. Her face was tomato red. She burrowed it into her hands as her shoulders shook. The woman beside her touched Melanie's shoulder, but Melanie shook it off and ran headlong toward her father. She burrowed against him—her safety net, her original home—and continued to cry.

The man wearing black who'd been giving the speech looked deflated. His eyes flashed with anger.

"Everyone, pack up! We're going back!" he called.

But it was too late.

A few other girls stepped out of the crowd, peering through the group, searching for their parents, their brothers, their family. One girl picked up her skirt and ran headlong toward her mother, throwing her arms around her.

It was as though a hypnosis was broken.

Maybe they've been homesick the entire time.

Still, Catherine searched the crowd for Ivy. It was pandemonium. She linked her hand with Quentin's and charged forward.

All the while, Scarlet had her camera raised. She was filming as tears rolled down her cheeks.

Chapter Twenty-Two

Scarlet recognized the man who'd been making a speech. He was the same man who'd whacked the front window of her car. Angry, deflated after the group of families had accosted them on the beach, he turned his back and wrapped his arms around a young woman with jet-black hair.

It felt like a stone in Scarlet's belly.

That's Ivy's boyfriend. She just knew.

Now that the police recognized what a monstrosity this all was, they were calling for backup. She heard one of them say, "We're going to need psychologists. Therapists. Can we call them in from Boston?"

"I'll call the chief," another said.

Scarlet was able to capture the entire scene on camera.

She lost Nathan in the chaos. His sister had seen him and raced toward him. He wept and led her to their parents, and now, they stood in a group hug as a family. Scarlet's camera lingered on the scene for a long moment. She wasn't sure if something so personal would make it in the final cut, but she knew Nathan would want to see it. *They'll welcome him back with open arms,* she thought. *But he still won't take their money.*

Together, Catherine, Quentin, James, and Scarlet approached Ivy.

Why did it take Ivy so long to join them? Scarlet wondered.

But she knew. It was because Ivy loved her family. It had taken her boyfriend a very long time to convince her. Who knew why she'd ultimately given in? Who knew why anyone did? Perhaps it was the pressure of her approaching a new semester at university. Maybe it was the pressure of their family asking her *what are you going to do? Why didn't you get an internship? Should you write an article about that? Are you using your summer well?*

Ivy turned as her family approached. Scarlet's arms felt heavy with the camera. She wanted to throw it aside and take Ivy in her arms. She was supposed to protect her little sister, but she'd gotten swept up in her own art.

Unlike the others, Ivy wasn't wearing a long dress. She wore a simple pair of jeans and a T-shirt. *She hasn't fallen for it completely,* Scarlet thought.

Suddenly, Ivy burst away from her boyfriend and into the arms of her mother. Catherine and Quentin wrapped their arms around her as the bonfire cast its orange light across their faces. The boyfriend and the other men wearing black hung back; they looked despondent. The young women whose parents hadn't come were scattered across the beach. A few of them had begun to walk away from the fire but in the opposite direction to the house where they'd been living.

A few of the men had begun to disband, too.

"I'm sorry," Ivy cried into her mother's shoulder. "I was just so confused."

"Shh," Catherine breathed, sweeping her hand through Ivy's hair. "We all get confused sometimes. But we're here now. It's going to be all right. I promise you that."

* * *

Scarlet, Catherine, and Nathan were allowed to go to the police precinct as the police interviewed the young women and paired them up with the therapists readily available at this time of night. The place was crowded with parents and daughters. An officer came with a big box of sweatpants and T-shirts so that the girls could change if they wanted to. They took turns in the bathroom and returned looking like modern young women. They threw their dresses into the trash.

Scarlet asked a few young women if she could interview them for the documentary. The first was Felicity Fellini. Her mother didn't explain their connection to Felicity until the following week, which led Scarlet to rewatch the footage several more times.

But now, all Scarlet knew of Felicity was that she had the same last name as Scarlet's great-grandfather from Italy. *Maybe we were related in the old country,* Scarlet thought as she set up the camera.

Felicity was meek and tired. She looked very small in her sweats and T-shirt. Her parents, April and Rainer, were seated off to the left of Scarlet's shot, holding hands. Felicity sucked in her cheeks.

"It started out like a philosophical game," Felicity explained when Scarlet asked her to *tell her everything.* "I met Xavier outside the English department, and we started talking about the pressures of modern society. How we're expected to give and give and give of ourselves. I was so tired of studying and keeping up with this big course load. And he said he was tired, too. I didn't learn till later that he wasn't even enrolled at Columbia. I just assumed what I wanted to assume. It didn't take long before I was head over heels for him. That's when he introduced me to other people around our age who spoke like him; who spoke about another way of living. They talked about freedom like it was a thing you could really have. That intrigued me. I always thought of myself as an outside thinker."

Felicity sniffed and pressed her hands over her eyes. "It will take me a while not to think the way they taught me to think."

"That's the way these people operate," Scarlet assured her.

Felicity sighed and removed her hands from her eyes again. "They told me that I was born in a prison of wealth. They told me I had to break out of it. They didn't let us communicate with our parents or anyone from the outside. I questioned it at first, but it just seemed so...so easy." Felicity rolled her shoulders back. "I'm so embarrassed to admit this."

"Don't be," Scarlet urged. "Does that mean they took your phones?"

"Yes. They did." Felicity furrowed her brow. "My dad just mentioned they texted our parents from our phones and asked for money." She wrapped her hand around her opposite wrist. "I don't really know what to say. I always thought I was a smart person. I can't believe I fell for this." Her brow crinkled up. "What is my great-grandma going to say? My great-grandfather came here from Italy—only for his great-granddaughter to fall in line with some kind of stupid cult?"

Felicity hung her head.

Scarlet did her best to assure Felicity that she wasn't stupid; that men like this were sophisticated in their attacks, and that the world wasn't always a cruel place. But Scarlet knew Felicity needed time to heal and be with her family.

April and Rainer soon gathered their daughter up and took her away. Scarlet imagined them later, sitting quietly in an ornate room. She hoped they'd find new ways to talk to each other. She hoped they'd find ways to be honest and show their tremendous love.

Wealth is a prison, Scarlet thought. *But it shouldn't be a prison that keeps us away from each other.*

April hugged Catherine hard before they disappeared into the darkness. "You'll let us know if you need anything else for your book," she said.

"I will," Catherine said.

Scarlet gave Catherine a funny look as she approached. "You went to the Fellinis about your book? The one about great-grandpa?"

"I did."

"Does that mean they really are related to us?" Scarlet asked.

Catherine looked tremendously tired. She sat in the plastic chair beside Scarlet and rubbed her knees. Scarlet realized she wasn't going to get an answer right then. Her mother's mind was elsewhere.

Ivy had been talking to a police officer for the better part of twenty minutes. They'd realized she was the most recent of the disappeared young women. She'd held out the longest before joining.

It meant her mind was still mostly of the real world, rather than the other one built up by the men wearing black. It meant she could give them the best information about what had really gone on—without tripping up on ideologies and fears.

The police hadn't been able to bring any of the men into custody. Scarlet knew it would be difficult to round them up. But because it was an island, the cops already had people watching the harbor and the ferry boats. It was to be a fascinating hunt to watch.

The door burst open to return Ivy to the lobby. Her shoulders were slumped; her eyes were lined with red. But already, Quentin and Catherine raced for her and wrapped her in a hug. Scarlet filmed for a few seconds, then turned the camera off and joined her family.

Scarlet's phone buzzed with a text from Nathan. They were already safe at his parents' place in Nantucket. He planned to spend the night.

NATHAN: Thank you for everything.

NATHAN: It's strangely great to be back with them.

NATHAN: None of this could have happened if you hadn't started digging around.

SCARLET: It couldn't have happened without your help, either.

Not long after that, Quentin drove them back home. James continued to cry in the back seat, too overwhelmed with emotions to say much of anything except, "I'm just so relieved."

Catherine said they'd talk more tomorrow. "But everyone needs to sleep," she ordered.

Scarlet and Ivy went upstairs to the room painted lilac and changed into big T-shirts. Scarlet's heart broke every time she looked at her little sister. *How could she have run away?*

Did I miss the signs?

Should I have helped her before it was too late?

But she was back. Scarlet didn't want to fixate on the past.

Ivy and Scarlet sat on Scarlet's bed, their feet hanging off and their backs against the chilly wall. Scarlet played music softly from her phone. Ivy looked fourteen or fifteen with her makeup off and her hair in a ponytail.

"I feel so stupid," Ivy said, her eyes to her toes.

"Don't."

Ivy placed her head on Scarlet's shoulder. Scarlet focused on her breath.

"Did you really love that guy?" Scarlet asked.

"I think so. I don't know." Ivy tried to laugh, but it sounded false. "What does anyone know about love, anyway?"

"Where did you meet him?"

"I met him here in Nantucket. Like I told you," Ivy said. "He made it seem like he was going to Columbia at first. I thought we were on the same page. And we had a lot of fun. We talked about everything. But looking back, I can see the little ways he tried to manipulate me. He belittled my education. He belittled my goals and dreams. And because I was falling in love with him, I let him do it.

I began to believe he was right." Ivy closed her eyes. "It sounds like such a cliché, doesn't it?"

Scarlet brushed Ivy's hair behind her ear. She remembered Owen, who'd manipulated her in a thousand different ways. She'd still loved him for years.

"You know I can't judge you," Scarlet reminded her.

Ivy was quiet for a moment.

"Not only that," Scarlet said, "I would never judge you. You're my sister, and I love you. I will always have empathy for your lived experience. I will always take your word above everyone else's."

Ivy sniffed and raised her head. Scarlet wanted to ask her, *Were you going to wear the long dresses? Were you going to give in?*

Why? What was it about that ideology? What was it about giving up on the real world that appealed to you so much?

But she knew the reason.

Everyone wanted to believe in a better world. Everyone wanted to believe they could find their way out of boredom or fear or hard work.

It wasn't dissimilar from their great-grandpa Gionnocaro. He'd imagined America to be this better and brighter world across the Atlantic—so far away from the war. But before he'd arrived, he'd lost everything. He'd had to make do with what he could.

"Are you going back to school?" Scarlet asked quietly. She sensed Ivy was nearly asleep.

Ivy's voice was like a string. "Do you think I should?"

It was clear going back frightened her. Maybe she didn't trust herself.

"I'll visit you all the time," Scarlet breathed. "We can go to our favorite diners and read at the park and go shopping. We can decide how to love the city as adults, rather than children."

Ivy sniffed. "But you're not coming back."

Scarlet shook her head.

Ivy pulled back and looked Scarlet in the eye. "I heard you mention something about a documentary. You're making it about us."

Scarlet nodded.

Ivy set her jaw. "Let me know what you need. I'll tell you anything. I'll give you anything you need."

Scarlet's heart swelled. She thanked her sister and watched as Ivy tiptoed across the room to turn off the light.

There in the dark, Scarlet realized something. Her documentary was going to be a very big deal.

Her career was on the brink.

She had to brace herself.

She had to hold on.

But she needed Nathan with her if she was really going to go for it. She made up her mind to tell him how she felt—both professionally and personally.

She couldn't keep it to herself a moment more.

Chapter Twenty-Three

Two weeks later, Catherine returned to New York City as a guest of the Fellini family. Scarlet came with her, armed with baked goods and little gifts for Ivy, with whom she planned to stay that night and maybe the one after that, depending on how the trip went. It was September, unseasonably chilly, and they bundled up in sweaters and drove south to that miraculous city. A city that had given them so much. A city that wasn't quite done with them yet, despite their departure.

Ivy met them on the street. She wore a vintage leather jacket and shiny lipgloss and had gained maybe a pound or two since the Nantucket incident—healthy weight that made her smile brighter and her eyes lighter. Catherine's eyes filled as her daughters embraced. Sometimes it was difficult for Catherine to face the facts of the recent past. But, she reckoned, if she was really a journalist, she had to find ways to carry all kinds of truths. Even modern ones about her family.

Catherine bought the girls lunch and fell into easy,

sweet gossip about Ivy's classes, her friends, and a boy who'd recently flirted with her in a linguistics class. It thrilled Catherine to hear she was doing so well. But she'd also promised to stay extra vigilant—to call her daughter frequently and ask if the pressure on her shoulders was too great.

There's no race in the finish line of life, she'd told Ivy before she'd gone back to school. *Take a breather if you need to. Listen to your body.*

Ivy had promised she would.

Ivy took a french fry and waved it over the table at the lunch spot they'd once frequented when the girls were small. Catherine assumed neither of them remembered that. She decided to keep the fact to herself.

"But tell me about Nathan," Ivy instructed Scarlet now.

Scarlet's cheeks went red. She stared into the basket of french fries as though they might give her an answer.

"You don't have to," Catherine said quietly. "I know it's still new."

Scarlet waved her hand. "I want to be open about it. I do." She shot Ivy a look, adding, "No more secrets between us."

Ivy gave a firm nod.

"When I first saw Nathan a few weeks ago, I knew something was about to happen," Scarlet admitted. "It felt like we were building a story together. At first, I thought maybe that story was just the documentary. But now, I don't know."

"Is he still staying with you?" Ivy asked.

Scarlet shook her head. "He returned to the city for a while to be with his family. But we're still working together and sharing footage. Talking about where to take the documentary. His sister and his parents have agreed to give an interview." Scarlet dotted her lips with a napkin. "But we have future ideas, too. Other documentaries. Other fiction films. Now that he doesn't work three jobs to make rent, it's like his creative mind is alive again. And we're applying for grants and things like that so money won't be an issue."

Scarlet smiled at Catherine. Catherine had already translated just how proud of Scarlet she was for refusing her family's money. She wanted to do it all on her own.

My children are my true legacy, Catherine thought.

After lunch, Catherine, Ivy, and Scarlet went for a long walk through Central Park, then returned to Ivy's apartment so the girls could regroup and talk about what they wanted to do later. Catherine changed into a sleek black dress and fixed her makeup in the bathroom mirror. She wanted to look the part for her visit with the Fellini family. She'd learned Dee was going to be there. She'd decided to lay her cards on the table.

She was frightened. Her hands were slick. But, she reasoned, she had nothing to lose. She and the Fellinis had very nearly lost everything in the here and now. The story of Gionnocaro One and Gionnocaro Two was entrenched in the past. It mattered very little.

It only mattered for the pages of Catherine's book.

Catherine left her car near Ivy's apartment and took a cab up to the Upper West Side so she didn't have to deal with parking. Once outside that illustrious building, she got onto the sidewalk and waved hello to the doorman. He was the same as ever. Catherine wondered if he ever had a day off. Maybe he was too proud to take one.

Catherine took the elevator to the penthouse apartment and walked into the open arms of April, her new friend. April smelled like smoke and rose—an exquisite, autumnal perfume. Rainer wheeled Stephan into the living room to say hello. Stephan wore a boisterous smile.

"You brought my granddaughter home," he said, taking both of Catherine's hands. "You're a friend of the Fellini family forever."

Even if my grandmother and grandfather killed your father? Catherine wondered.

Very soon after Catherine arrived, Rainer left to collect Dee from the Elder Care Home. Throughout his absence, April explained how they'd handled the past two weeks as a family.

"Felicity is taking the semester off to regroup and go to therapy." April smiled. "It's funny how easy it is to say that. A year ago, I would have lied before saying my daughter needed therapy. But Rainer and I have lately spoken so often about approaching life with honesty and optimism. We don't want to hide anymore. Maybe it was that sense of hiding away that forced Felicity away from us in the first place."

Catherine raised her shoulders. "I've thought the same about Ivy."

April explained that Felicity was attending an all-weekend retreat in Upstate New York for victims of manipulation. "It's going to take some rewiring, but they think she'll be okay," April said. "She's already spoken about being a potential spokesperson for this kind of thing. She said, 'Mom, I always thought I was too smart for something like this. It proves how easy it is for young women to get swept up.' I feel so proud of her. The work your eldest is doing on the documentary is also essential to Felicity's mission."

Catherine smiled. "They're extraordinary."

April went on to say that the cops were looking into the funds that had been stolen from the parents of the young women.

"Every woman involved gave a statement that their phones were taken away from them. That means the young men were imitating them to get the cash from us parents," April said. "That's a federal crime. It's possible we'll go to court."

"Let me know how I can help," Catherine said.

"You've done enough," April assured her. "But thank you."

Dee arrived not long after that. Unlike last time, she required no walker to move around. She walked regally, bowing down to kiss her son Stephan on the cheek, then taking Catherine's hand in hers and smiling.

"It's just wonderful what you've done for my family," Dee said.

Catherine stood and kissed Dee on the cheek. She wanted to burst with what she knew about Gwen. Her heart swelled.

But already, April urged them all to sit. The cake and coffee were ready. The champagne needed to be popped and poured.

Catherine stood with her flute glass filled with bubbly. She met Dee's gaze.

"A toast to Catherine, the journalist," Dee said.

"To Catherine!" the rest of the Fellini family celebrated.

Catherine felt a blush crawl up her arms and across her chest. They sat down, and she struggled not to stare at Dee. To her, Dee seemed to carry a wealth of secrets. *Would she ever give them up?*

"I think it's lovely my great-granddaughter will take some time off," Dee announced.

April perked up. She looked surprised.

"I've noticed the tremendous pressure on young women today," Dee said. "They're expected to be everything at once. Back when I first went to school, I knew what I was getting into. I knew there would be no help from my husband when it came to childrearing. Of course, I had hired help. But it wasn't the same. I hardly slept." Dee studied the tips of her French nails. She spoke as though it was about somebody else's life.

"Tell Felicity to come by the home soon," Dee instructed her grandson. "I'd love to talk to her more about the things that matter. Art and beauty and literature and music. We are given so little time on this earth, and these are the things that make that time worth living. I need her to remember that again."

Dee's voice cracked just the slightest bit. It was the only proof that there was any emotion behind that gorgeous and formidable face.

It's her facade. She's too practiced in keeping it up to ever let it fall, Catherine thought.

Dee turned her attention to Catherine. A shadow passed over her face. For a long moment, Catherine and Dee looked at one another in the eye. Catherine knew better than to break eye contact. Dee called the shots now.

Dee's lips parted. Then she whispered, "Of course. You really do look so much like her."

Catherine's heart shifted. *She sees Gwen in my face.*

"Like who, Mom?" Stephan asked.

But Dee was the only one who knew. Her eyes were

strange. She took a long sip of champagne. "My goodness."

Catherine dared a response. "She was my grandmother."

Dee's eyes filled with tears. She blinked them away. "My goodness," she said again.

"Who was your grandmother?" April asked. She turned her eyes from Catherine to Dee and back again.

Secrets and lies hung in the air between all of them.

Dee waved her hand. "Catherine and I need the room."

Everyone was taken aback. Rainer's face went blank. Stephan touched the wheels of his chair and furrowed his brow.

But Dee had ordered it. She was the matriarch. She called the shots.

April burst from her chair and wheeled Stephan down the hall, calling back for Rainer to follow. "We'll be in the music room," she said. "Just knock when you're ready for us."

Suddenly, it was only Dee and Catherine in the room. Dee and Catherine and all those secrets.

Dee picked up the bottle of champagne and refilled her glass, then reached over to refill Catherine's. Catherine couldn't breathe. She felt as though she'd traversed continents to get here.

"Gwen was your grandmother," Dee whispered. Her hand found her heart. "Gwen was my very best friend in the world."

Catherine swallowed. She didn't dare speak.

"It means he was your grandfather," Dee added. "The other Gionnocaro Fellini."

"I don't understand," Catherine breathed. "Your son

and your grandson told me stories about your Gionnocaro. They were the same stories my grandfather used to tell me."

Dee's face broke into a beautiful smile. "He kept telling them?"

"Until he died," Catherine said.

Dee leaned back in her chair and crossed her ankles. She looked beautiful.

"I've never told this story before," she said.

Catherine raised her chin. She wasn't sure if she would ever be allowed to tell this story to anyone else. Maybe she wouldn't be able to write her book.

But at least she'd know the truth.

"I've already told you that my Gionnocaro wasn't the brightest star in the universe," Dee began. "He was often an idiot and never a very good academic. I taught him everything I knew. But the problem was, he was incredibly charismatic. Everywhere he went, people loved him. *I* loved him. More than anything. For a little while." Dee's smile fell. "But even before we got married, he showed me how cruel he could be. Italy seemed like a very backward place. Men openly hit their wives. Women did everything in service of them. I think he expected me to be both at once. He wanted me to be the academic who taught him everything, but he also wanted me to cook and clean and deliver children. I felt I was juggling the world, the moon, and Saturn all at once. In fact, Felicity's story with these young men was very familiar to me. I understand what it was like to be manipulated. It was like having your heart ripped out and reanimated.

"Back then, I hired Gwen to work for us because Gwen had very little and hadn't been allowed to attend university right away. I just adored her. I adored having her close. She saw firsthand what kind of man Gionno-caro was. She hated him! Every time he started telling another of his stories, she went about slamming doors and cleaning angrily. It cracked me up. But I told her to be careful. I didn't want Gionnocaro to strike her."

Dee pulled her lips into a sad smile. "I have a feeling you think there's a murder at the end of this story. I'm sorry to disappoint you. Gionnocaro's death was an accident in the truest sense. He was drinking. He fell down the stairs and hit his head." Dee snapped her fingers. "Just like the papers say, I was in the Hamptons with the children and Gwen at the time. We came back to tend to things. We weren't sure what to do.

"By then, Gwen was seeing a young man she'd met in the Upper East Side at a jazz club. He was Jewish and incredibly damaged after what he'd seen in Europe. He'd escaped by the hair of his chin," Dee said. "His wife and two of his children had been taken to the camps and killed there. And he genuinely believed he should have died, too. By 1945, he was in the midst of an identity crisis. He was terrified. He loved Gwen, but he needed to start over." Dee raised her shoulders. "So I gave Gwen some money. I gave her Gionnocaro's papers. I gave her a new identity that Joseph could run with."

Catherine's jaw hung open. Tears flowed freely.

"I knew we couldn't see each other much after that," Dee said. "But she wrote me often from the other side of the park. She and the new Gionnocaro started a bakery together. They had children—sensational children who went on to do brilliant things. The new Gionnocaro no longer clung to his past. He told stories about a royal life in Italy. He put his history to bed."

Catherine was on her feet. She clutched her flute of

champagne with stiff fingers. She thought she might faint.

"So you see?" Dee said with a soft smile. "Your grandfather Gionnocaro could begin anew in America—all because of the stupid death of my arrogant husband. I suppose that makes the two of us linked forever. Doesn't it? Oh, but what matters is we have our families. Who gives a crap about history as long as we have love."

* * *

Catherine confessed the story to Scarlet and Ivy the following morning over bacon, egg, and cheese sandwiches. Scarlet and Ivy didn't ask a single question. They gaped at her as though she'd lost her mind.

"He lost his children," Scarlet breathed finally, tightening her arms over her chest. "He lost his first wife."

The truth of that hung over their table like a cloud.

He left such devastation behind. He built something out of the horror of his life. And that's the only reason any of us are here.

Catherine convinced her girls to go to Ellis Island one last time. She wanted to find Joseph deVries.

Again, they waited in line for forty-five minutes between other families whose ancestors had floated across the Atlantic to make something new of themselves. What united them was hope—or maybe just the memory of that hope.

It didn't take long for Catherine, Ivy, and Scarlet to find the photograph of Joseph deVries. In his photograph, he looked sad and broken; the light had gone out from his eyes. When Catherine compared this photo to future photos of her grandfather—after he'd become Gionnocaro

Fellini—she realized he'd breathed new life into himself. His eyes were alight. He had a family. He had a new life.

"Hi, Grandpa," Catherine breathed to the photo as she captured it on her phone. "We found you. And we love you. No matter what you're called."

* * *

Coming Next in the Nantucket Sunset Series
Pre Order Nantucket Gala

Other Books by Katie

The Vineyard Sunset Series

A Nantucket Sunset Series

Secrets of Mackinac Island Series

Sisters of Edgartown Series

A Katama Bay Series

A Mount Desert Island Series

The Coleman Series

The Salt Sisters

The Sutton Book Club

A Frosty Season Series